Ruckus A

Revised Version

Hope you enjoy.
Thanks,
Barbara Barton

True Tales of Early Settlements along Spring Creek, Dove Creek and the Concho Rivers

By Barbara Barton

Present Day Map of Three River Area with Highways

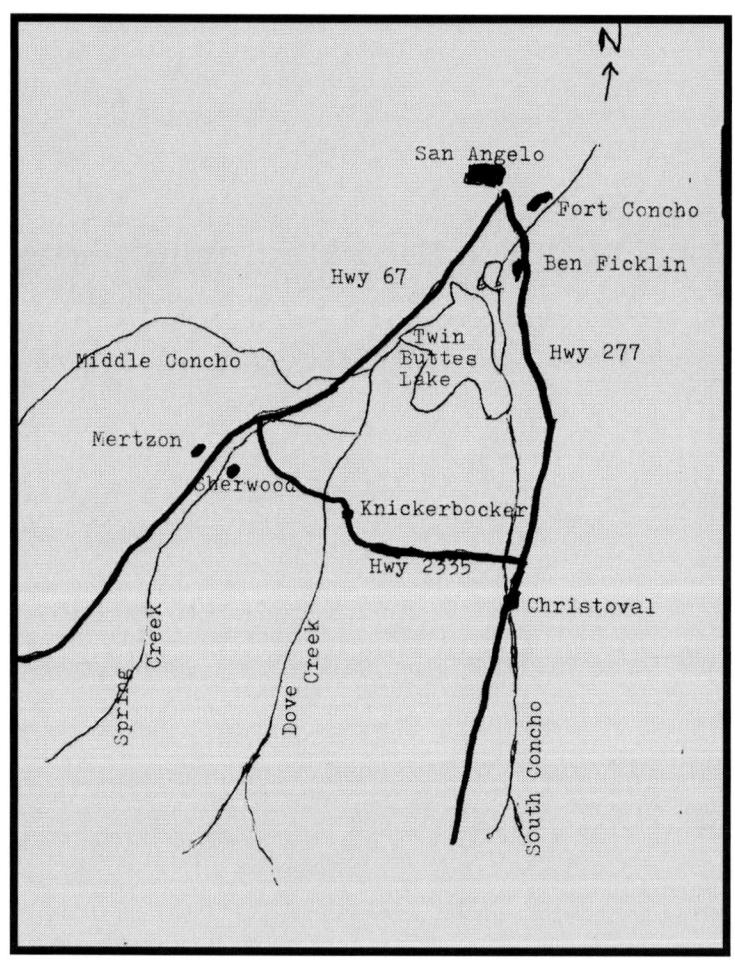

ISBN 0-943639-28-X

First Edition 1997

Second Edition 1998

Third Edition March 1999

Revised Edition January, 2010

Printed by Barton's Books

Box 6

Knickerbocker, TX 76939

BB7303@AOL.COM

325-949-7303

Other books by Barbara Barton:

Den of Outlaws,

Saber, Shield & Spurs

Stagecoach Lines & Freighters of West Texas

Secrets of the Sherwood Courthouse

Ben Ficklin

Pistol Packin' Preachers

Contents

PREFACE

The ruckus or commotion caused by little towns emerging in the late 1800s along the rivers in Concho country is the heart of this book. Early settlers fought Indians, the weather and each other in those first years.

Since the communities existing on South Concho, Dove Creek and Spring Creek have been a big part of my life, I wanted to write about their early settlement. I grew up in Sherwood and played along Spring Creek as a kid. Christoval Schools allowed me to teach math and science there for 19 years, so that community has a warm spot in my heart also. My science classes went on field trips along the Concho River. My husband Lewis and I have lived over forty years on Dove Creek near Knickerbocker, so it's special too. I feel that I have close ties to all three areas.

Early Indian grinding holes in the rocks along the rivers whetted my appetite to know more about the Indians along these streams. I have used some material from Dr. Frankie Beth Nelson's talk on the Lipan Apaches, which she gave at Fort Concho's Spring Lecture Series. I live about eight miles from the site of the Dove Creek Battle between Texas troops and the Kickapoo Indians in 1865. Archives at Fort Concho National Historic Landmark were an asset in this study of the battle. As I began to research early Indian movements in this area, I was amazed to find that famous Robert E. Lee spent some of his time chasing Indians across this country.

Personal interviews have been a lot of fun during this search for information. Some people, who had outlaws for ancestors, delighted in telling about them. Other descendants of the outlaws were defensive when asked to discuss their distant relatives. This three rivers area certainly had its share of outlaws.

The Black Jack Ketchum gang originated in Knickerbocker but circulated in the Christoval and Sherwood areas as well. Dave Atkins shot Tom Hardin in a saloon in Knickerbocker and stayed in hiding around the nearby hills for years. Laura Bullion grew up on a ranch between Knickerbocker and Sherwood before she left with Ben Kilpatrick and the Wild Bunch. They robbed trains as far away as Montana.

In my research, I visited the ranch homes of Black Jack and Laura Bullion, as well as Black Jack's first hideout. I also interviewed family members of the two outlaws. Although the outlaw trail was interesting, the bulk of this story tells about good, solid frontier men and women searching for a new home. They left a legacy of hard work and high morals in this land they loved.

The Concho Country was a melting pot of different nationalities. Whereas W. C. Jones came to Christoval from Wales, Joseph Tweedy of Knickerbocker had ancestors in New York and Scotland. The Thomas Jacques and Barnabe Martinez families came from Spain and Mexico. Each person brought rich traditions and experiences with them.

I want to thank many people who helped me along the trails of this research: Suzanne Campbell at the West Texas Collection at ASU for help with pictures; my sister Sharon Gentry who sketched some outlaws; Ross McSwain for giving helpful suggestions; Norma Gentry and Ken Hodgson for proof-reading; the people who allowed me to interview them; Billie Marie Van Court for pictures; Katherine Waring, Betty Sykes and Rose Duke for helping me with local history; DeWitt Ayers for being my guide at the Battle of Dove Creek site and the Byler Ranch; and my husband Lewis for his patience and understanding.

Chapter 1 –Indians before the Ruckus

Peaceful Lipan Apaches and Kickapoo Indians couldn't imagine the abrupt changes, which would soon take place in their mid-1800s environment. They saw the peaceful streams we call Dove Creek, Concho River and Spring Creek as a sanctuary with grass stirrup high on the rolling hills. They had no idea that settlers would soon change their life, as well as the life of the buffalo forever.

Lipan Apaches were a short, round-headed tribe found in the Concho River area. Surprisingly, the Lipan women were the head of the household. These women cooked the food and let their daughters take some to their own families. The Lipans believed in ghosts, evil spirits, and witches, but were very gentle to nature's living things. They often asked forgiveness for bending a bush or killing an animal.

The young Lipans had definite steps in their life. First they lived in a cradle-board until they were old enough to walk. At this time, the ceremony of first steps then took place. In the next stage of their life, the four and five-year-old children had to run up a mountain every morning to make them tough. Swimming was important, so they were thrown in the water and made to paddle to survive. At puberty a girl was covered with five cups of pollen as a ritual.

The Lipans became more mobile when they obtained horses from the Spaniards and fought against the Comanches. Texans tried to make friends with the Lipans and protect them from the fierce Comanches. When Spaniards or Indians won a battle, they took slaves. The Lipans had slaves, including children. They worked them very hard, but did adopt them as their very own family members. This tribe even helped some of the first settlers when they arrived.

Santana, a Kiowa Chief lead his tribe during the time that West Texas was settling. Courtesy of the Library of Congress.

Another tribe that moved around West Texas in the 1800s was the Kiowas. Santana was their chief who lead them in battles against the white man, as well as forays to raid them of their cattle.

One early white man to see this area was Robert E. Lee with his troops when he chased Indians in West Texas. As he reined in his horse and wiped the caked dust from his face, he felt the dry summer winds of West Texas parch his whole body.

This country where he was trailing Indians was quite different from his beloved Virginia. In 1856 he had been assigned to Camp Cooper, which was in Throckmorton County. The Indian renegade Sanaco had escaped a reservation in northern Texas and headed west with a band of his men. Lee's mission was to capture him.

Robert E. Lee learned to chase Indians in West Texas. Courtesy of the Library of Congress.

As the chase grew longer, Lee found himself in the Concho Valley. He led his troops toward the Middle Concho River and westward. Each time he found sign of their camp, Sanaco was a day ahead of the troops. Finally, near present day Big Springs, Lee's men got close enough to the Indians that the "redmen" were afraid of capture. The runaways set a grass fire. As Lee's men tried to chase the Indians and go around the fire, they were almost killed. From the soldier's description, the fire covered about 50 counties as the land is divided today.

Lee's men were scorched from the fire and unrelenting heat of that summer. They traveled 1,100 miles in 40 days but never caught Sanaco and his band. Lee wasn't very impressed by the Middle Concho area as he traveled through this inferno. The troops finally made it back to Camp Cooper but were a burned, thirsty group.

By 1861, many settlers were pushing toward West Texas in spite of Indians led by Sanaco. Several elements made life dangerous in the new west. In addition to Indians moving about, thieves, robbers and renegades were also on the loose. This need for protection brought about the formation of the Minute Men. They had to be of good character, willing to scout one-fourth of the time and not be away from home more than two months at a time.

In December of 1863, the state of Texas organized the Ranger Service. Some Minute Men became a part of this service. They served one-forth of their time with the troops and the rest could be used at home, were paid two-dollars and twenty-five cents a day, and furnished their own equipment. Outlaws and Indians were their main focus.

One such fighter figured into the settling of the Concho country. Richard Tankersley served as a Minute Man from

Brown County. In 1858, he saw the Concho country while on a scouting trip. He said, "The country I saw was beautiful. The hills were green with waving grass, the streams were full of fish and game like buffalo and antelope were common."

Tankersley moved his family to the head of the South Concho in 1864. His family traveled in a wagon pulled by oxen as they followed his herd of cattle. Annie and Richard had four children at this time and one on the way. Fayette, the oldest child, was not old enough to help his father very much with the cattle, so this cattle drive was a one-man affair. Richard stopped near the springs of the South Concho and built a cabin and corral for his livestock. Since there were no neighbors nearby, the Tankersleys had few visitors.

On a cold day in January of 1865, the Tankersleys saw several Indians walking up the path to their home. Richard grabbed his gun to protect his family, but soon realized that the Indians were friendly Kickapoo. When Tankersley welcomed them into his house he said, "They went through the house, opening drawers and looking at everything, but didn't take anything." Mrs. Tankersley remembered her manners as a hostess, so she offered them fresh honey from the comb. One brave said they were camping at Dove Creek and had lost some horses. Tankersley told him that he had some missing also. Both men agreed to look for the other's horses and the Indians left. The next morning Richard was delighted to see one of his missing horses in his corral. Tankersley didn't know that this particular chief and his tribe had been under observation by U. S. soldiers for some time.

Days before Tankersley met the Indians, Captain N. W.

Richard F. Tankersley settled along the South Concho River. Courtesy of Fort Concho Historical Landmark.

Gillintine of the Second Frontier District at Gatesville, Coryell County, had taken 23 men with him on a scouting patrol. They discovered an abandoned Indian camp on the Clear Fork of the Brazos on December 9, 1864. He predicted some 500 or more Indians in the band. Other accounts show Captain Gillintine with a company of frontier scouts predicting some 4,000 Indians.

Both stories indicated that they were hostile Indians and needed to be followed. No one tried to check with the Indians to see if they were peaceful. Instead, the soldiers spied on them and determined them to be hostile, maybe being led by Union

"Jayhawkers." Reports were even made that these Indians intended to winter here and attack the white settlements as soon as warmer weather arrived.

Rumors of Yankee-Indian invasion flashed from settlement to settlement. The troops who followed the Indian trail were composed of Confederate men and state militia. Forces of Col. J. B. Barry from Fort Belknap and Capt. Jack Currenton of Palo Pinto County made up the 200 Confederate soldiers.

Militia from Erath, Brown, Comanche and Parker counties made up the 200 men. The militia was under the command of Captain S. S. Totten. All 400 men would be under the command of Captain John Fossett of Camp Colorado. Totten was a former Confederate soldier himself. After being discharged from the military due to wounds, Captain Totten got back into the saddle to lead the militia. His troops described him as "sour in disposition, but thorough as a disciplinarian." To further complicate matters, Totten had never fought large numbers of enemies. His men said, "Captain Totten is vain and insecure."

Totten did want his men to have better fire power than they had, so on December the 17th he rode to Waco and purchased 6,000 percussion caps. He also picked up some Tonks, Tonkawa Indians who could be used as guides. Details of this trip were given in the diary of L. H. Scruthfield who rode with Totten. This hurried trip was made in two days in a pouring, cold rain. Against orders, Totten proceeded not to Fort Chadbourne with his men, but went to where Gillintine had first seen the trail of the Indians and followed it all the way to Dove Creek.

While the militia was moving out, the Confederate troops were preparing to leave from Camp Colorado. Wagons couldn't be used to carry provisions because the country the soldiers were going to was wild with the only inhabitants being buffalo, wolves and prairie dogs. No roads were available, so food and ammunition were loaded onto some pack mules. From Camp Colorado, which was located in the northern part of present-day Coleman County, Barry's men marched to Fort Chadbourne where they were met by Captain Currenton. He had continued to track the Indians, which he said was easy because their trail was 50 to 60 yards wide. He showed Barry's men another deserted village the Indians left behind.

The troops dismounted to look over the deserted village of some 375 wigwams. Framework made of willow branches still stood where the buffalo hides once covered them. These wigwams should have been a hint that these particular Indians were friendly because the hostile Kiowas and Comanches didn't have such wigwams.

Barry's troops camped at the North Fork of the Concho River after going over mountainous trails for two days. The Indians had camped at this point earlier and their wigwams numbered 500, which was an increase over the first estimate of the camp. Soldiers also found near the abandoned camp a tree that had been cut with an axe to make a target. These Indians, which the soldiers were tracking, had target practice with guns, not bows and arrows.

The soldiers could see that the Indians were headed west toward the Middle Concho River, so the Confederate troops decided to wait for the Militia at Ranger Spring near present day Water Valley. After six days of waiting, Totten didn't show up, and the scouts had not returned. Fossett became impatient and left a note for Totten on the trail. He commanded his soldiers to forge on toward the Indians. The note said:

Headquarters, Northern Concho, January 7, 1865

Captain Totten,

Commanding State Militia

Dear Sir:

Having waited here on the North Concho for six days to enable you to overtake this command, we go forward this morning on the trail of the Indians. We will probably camp on the Middle Fork of the Concho tonight; your assistance is greatly needed; make all haste to overtake us: my scouts have not been heard from for the past week. I fear they have been killed.

John Fossett,

Commanding

A day later his scouts met them to tell them of a large Indian encampment on Dove Creek, a tributary of the Middle Concho. The Indians had 6,000 horses and many wigwams, but the name of the tribe couldn't be determined. Strange as it seems, at this point Fossett decided that his 200 men could defeat this large band of Indian braves without waiting for Capt.

Totten. The fact that the Indians had rifles didn't slow him down either. He also did not know if they were hostile Indians, or friendly, but that factor didn't seem to matter to him.

Fossett's scouts saw the Kickapoo Indian encampment on Dove Creek about January 7, 1865. After planning the attack for the next day, Fossett lead his troops to the Middle Concho so they could "shoot off their guns, clean them and reload. With out the Indians hearing the noise," according to I.B. Ferguson, one of the Confederate soldiers. During the night, three of Totten's men rode into their camp on the Middle Concho, and said that they had found the note that Fossett left for them.

Now the united forces could be used for the attack the next day. Fossett told the three messengers to return to Totten and tell him to bring his men immediately since his forces would attack the following morning. Totten's men were given a guide who had seen the Indian camp and could lead them to the rendezvous point one mile north of the Indian camp.

The next morning, January 8, 1865, when the "Flop-eared militia" finally appeared, it was already 9 o'clock. These troops carried this name because they had all kinds of firearms: shotguns, squirrel rifles, muskets and pistols. Final plans were made very hurriedly between Fossett and Totten. The Indians were camped on the east side of Dove Creek, about 10 miles from where Dove Creek joined Spring Creek. Totten's militia were to cross Dove Creek and attack straight on; whereas Fossett was to circle the hill and come from the behind the Indians. Totten described the Indian camp: It was a dense thicket of green briars and live oak, containing about 100 acres.

The creek was in front of a high bluff with heavy timber at its base; in their rear there were two dry branches in the thicket that were completely concealed by brush and briars, forming the best of rifle pits.

Totten lead the attack. As the militia came across Dove Creek, the Indians picked them off from their protected locations behind rocks and brush. Captain R. S. Barnes, William Culver and N. W. Gillintine were killed in the first wave of attack, along with 16 others. Quickly the Indians finished off the Texans and by 10 a.m. the militia was thrown in such a panic that they retreated north toward Spring Creek, never to be reckoned with in the battle again. Fossett's men hadn't even opened fire. He had divided his men along Dove Creek, one on the hill and one in the ravine.

Capt N.M. Gillintine was killed in the Dove Creek Battle, January 8, 1865. Courtesy of the West Texas Collection, Angelo State Univ.

From these positions, the Confederates held their battle line better and put up a stronger fight than the militia did. One action that worked in their favor was to capture the Indians' herd of horses early in the battle. Some of the Tonk scouts, who worked for the militia, moved the horses away from the fighting.

The Indians used the two streams, the dry ravine and Dove Creek, to their advantage. They moved through both places and stayed concealed until they were ready to open fire on the Confederates. In this way the soldiers were caught in a crossfire. As the fighting continued during the day, the troops realized they were badly outnumbered. Also during the course of the battle, prisoners were taken and the soldiers realized that they were fighting friendly Indians, the Kickapoo. Fossett's men decided the only thing they could do was to continue the fight until dark and try to retreat.

About thirty minutes before sundown, the soldiers selected a mount from the large number of Indians ponies they had captured. Each man who had lost a horse now could remount. The wounded soldiers were placed on the horses so they could travel also. Some of the men had to be tied onto their mounts. The plan was to move the herd of ponies first across Dove Creek, then the wounded, followed by the rear guard. The Kickapoo who were mounted were trying to cut off the horses. Suddenly the firing stopped until the herd got in position to ford the creek. Just at that instant the Indians on foot as well as horseback opened fire on the crossing herd.

The Kickapoo were able to recapture most of their stock. However, the troops were able to make a stand against them, so the wounded soldiers could retreat across the river unharmed.

Then the mounted Indians pursued the fleeing soldiers. Panic struck and no amount of officer commands could bring the troops back into control. Several troopers lost horses and were killed. Finally the Indians had driven the soldiers far from their camp, so they quit the pursuit. Gun shells and other relics from this retreat where found years later on land that was a mile or so from the battle. As the troops traveled the eight miles from Dove Creek to Spring Creek, they began to see many campfires along the river. The soldiers worried that they were coming into another Indian camp, but scouts reported back that the fires belonged to Totten's men. At last the troops could dismount and warm by a fire.

A short time after dark, a cold rain added to the troops' misery. It turned into sleet and then snow, so that on January 10, the ground was covered with about a foot of snow, the most white stuff that West Texas had seen in a long time. With nothing to eat and the wounded moaning during much of the night, the troopers decided to break camp next morning.

By attaching stretchers between the stirrups of two saddled horses, the sick men were carried. This way the hurt, frozen men started eastward on January the 11th to find civilization again. Although the initial count of dead soldiers consisted of 4 Confederate and 18 militia, the number was to increase on the way back because they were carrying 20 wounded.

Traveling conditions were terrible since food was nonexistent, frostbite was always a danger, and the horses were freezing to death. One young man named Jim Dyer had been shot in the stomach during the battle. The stumbling horses carrying his stretcher made him cry out in pain. As he died and was buried along the trail, a soldier named Ferguson later wrote,"Here by …this beautiful river sleeps the remains of this heroic boy who 'did not get home.'"

After three days on the trail, the sun came out and traveling was easier for the frozen soldiers. They overtook the Tonk scouts who still had about 250 of the Kickapoos' horses. Everybody now had a mount and some horses were slaughtered for food since no buffalo or other game was available to kill. The day they finally met up with their scouts was four days after the battle, and some men ate for the first time. They knew when the battle was over that their scouts had found the nearest help some 100 miles away at John Chisum's ranch at the mouth of the Concho. Getting to this ranch had been their goal since leaving Dove Creek. On the 17th of January, a weary bunch of troopers stumbled onto Chisum's ranch. There they were able to get 1,500 pounds of flour and all the beef they needed.

While at Chisum's ranch, another death took place. Doctors had to cut a rifle ball out of Lieutenant J. R. Brook's body the first night there. Brook was in so much pain that he knew the end was near. He requested Ferguson to write a letter to his wife, which the sick man was to dictate, as well as a will, before the end came. He was buried on the banks of the Concho River with honors of war. The return trip was complete when Camp

Colorado appeared on the horizon. The soldiers were glad to see this familiar site. Some troopers rode on to Fort Belknap where this encounter had started in the first place.

Totten returned to the site of the battle a short time later to find that the Indians had left in haste, abandoning some 1,000 buffalo hides, which could have been valuable for trading. Household gear such as 250 ovens or skillets and 200 saddles were scattered about on the deserted campsite. Totten also reported that there was evidence at the campsite that the Indians had been in contact with the Federals. Totten fully believed that come spring, these Indians with the Jayhawkers would "break up our frontier settlements."

After the battle at Dove Creek, the Kickapoo headed to the Mexican border and once there, thy banded with other Indians to raid ranches across the river into Texas. This raiding occurred for many years. In 1911 John Warren Hunter gave this Kickapoo version of the Battle of Dove Creek:

One chief carried a white cloth out to talk and they killed him. A young woman, Oo-lath-la-hi-na had gone to school at Fort Gibson. She could read and write. She said, "I will go out and talk with the white Captain. He thinks we are Comanches. The white men won't shoot a woman." She walked out to talk to them and they killed her. Then the Indians had to fight or stand and be killed like rabbits. That day the Kickapoo chief was No-ko-wat. He later stated that they lost 11 men and had 31 wounded.

This was one of the last few battles connected to the Civil War that was fought in Texas. Lee surrendered April 9th, but much bloodshed between Indians and white settlers continued for years, partially because of this attack on the Indians. Many questions concerning the battle go unanswered. Why did the soldiers not realize they were friendly Indians when they saw their wigwam poles, why attack when they knew the Indians were well armed with guns and outnumbered them, and why did Totten attack early instead of following Fossett's orders? The answers to these questions may lie in I. B. Ferguson's words in the heat of the battle. He said, "I had by this time learned that the boys had not killed all the Indians, that there were plenty of them left for me to kill, and I had all day to do it."

Fossett was held accountable for this unnecessary battle. The Army wanted to punish him, so an event unfolded which allowed this to happen. Capt. Henry Fossett supposedly gave verbal leave to Bugler Henry Lackey and his brother William to leave Camp Colorado August 17, 1864. They visited Gainsville, Texas, and were questioned by Col. Bourland's military police. They didn't have written orders, so they were arrested and taken to Camp Colorado.

The military used this incident to bring martial charges against Capt. Henry Fossett. They held him until May 31, 1865 at Fort Belknap, but he wasn't brought to trial. His incarceration was his punishment for starting the Dove Creek Battle. The Lackey boys survived this ordeal, and they appear in this story later in the Sherwood community development.

Chapter 2 – Christoval's Ruckus

After a long trip from his home in Kentucky, Washington (Wash) DeLong saw Texas through the eyes of a daring nineteen-year old looking for adventure. DeLong entered Texas by way of the Red River and by 1859 he had joined a frontier regiment to become a Minute Man like R. F. Tankersley. Fort Belknap, in north Texas, was where he had to report after each patrol.

His regiment had been fighting in the Indian Territory in 1860. After a long redman chase, DeLong returned to Belknap "weary, shaggy and loaded with scalps as well as other trophies." The other soldiers considered him a hero, but their admiration wasn't what interested DeLong. He had just caught sight of pretty Sylvinia Paralee Williams, who was helping to serve the food. After they got acquainted, her presence definitely made each trip back to Belknap something he anticipated.

As a Minute Man, DeLong made a trip to West Texas and fought in the Battle of Dove Creek. This experience didn't keep him out of West Texas because a couple of years later he traveled to the Concho country again, this time with Ed Love. While investigating Texas, they were attacked by seventeen Indians near present-day Christoval. DeLong was hit by a bullet that shattered his elbow. Luckily, he was a survivor of this encounter with Indians and returned to Fort Belknap. It took several years for him to win Sylvinia's hand, but they courted over a period of time and were married in April of 1865.

The newlyweds headed southwest to settle in a country where rivers flowed over the limestone and game was plentiful. They came to Lipan Springs, which is now in the Wall community area. They arrived in time for Christmas of 1866. The newly weds lived in a picket house and survived by ranching Durham cattle and selling milk, butter, eggs and chickens to the new army post nearby. As their children were born, the DeLong family didn't stay in one place too long. They moved to Kickapoo Springs for a time. Eventually they made one more move as they traveled along the South Concho. They saw deer, antelope, coyote, prairie chickens, grouse and plenty of prairie dogs.

The newly weds visited the territory that the Confederate troops under the direction of Captain Henry Fossett had viewed in May of 1865. At the time, they were chasing Confederate deserters. This was possible because Fossett wasn't jailed until three months later in August for his leadership in the Battle of Dove Creek. While traveling around the South Concho, his troops found several cabins built on Cole Creek, just south of modern-day Christoval. The deserters had left the cabins about a week before Fossett made his discovery in May.

Of course the Indians roamed freely through this land, so most settlers took their life in their own hands when they lived in this area of Texas. There was neither a fort nor soldiers for protection at the time the DeLongs settled on the fertile South Concho. Wash DeLong did have the help of his brothers Sam and Dave as they forged a farm out of the new land.

DeLong's first settlement along the South Concho was at the Christoval town site because he owned a section of land that included the town. He paid the hefty price of $13 for this tract of land, which he later said he traded for a wagon and a team of horses. Another version of the swap says he traded Christoval for three sections of land and 800 head of sheep.

Eventually, Wash moved about three miles from Christoval to a farm north of the community. He immediately began steps to remove irrigation water from the river. One can tell what was important to Wash DeLong because the irrigation system was built first, and their nice home was built later, about 1870. Lumber for the house was hauled by ox-cart from Austin. Sylviana was the envy of other women when they visited her because Mrs. DeLong's home had plank floors, and she had the first sewing machine in the area.

A cemetery developed near the DeLong house and is still there today. I counted eleven graves, most of which were related to the DeLong family. One grave outside the cemetery's chain-linked fence was that of John R. Gibson, 1819 to 1899. His tombstone said he was a veteran of the 1846 War. The location of this cemetery is near where the Knickerbocker Road intersects Highway 277.

As other families entered the valley made by the South Concho, military protection was needed more than ever. Solders from Fort Chadbourne and Fort Mason seldom ventured into the Concho country, so the settlers had no protection from the Indians. Concerned citizens met at the Ben Ficklin community. Jack Nabors said he would ride horseback the one hundred four miles to Fort Mason and urge that military protection for this area take place. Few citizens expected to see him alive again when he departed from home on the trip a few days later. Surprisingly he made it through the Indian infested area to the post. He voiced his concern rather convincingly, and Fort Concho became a reality in 1867.

Other families were settling along the South Concho, including the P.H. (Paddy) Mires family. They left Menard and traveled three days with wagon and team to get to the South Concho in the early 1870s. They settled about three miles out of present-day Christoval on the road now called Toe Nail Trail. The first thing Mires did was build a picket house near the springs, which flowed into the Concho River. A few years later, Jack Miller helped Paddy Mires build a beautiful two-story rock house on his place. Native limestone was used in the house, and remains of that home are still visible.

The Springs by the Mires House was so strong that Paddy built a grist mill and ground corn, wheat and grain for himself and his neighbors. His large house was a natural as a central meeting point in the area. Eventually the San Angelo-Sonora stage road passed by the Mires house. The family decided to use their home as a stage stop, so they took in weary stage riders and freighters.

Once a traveler and his son spent the night at the Mires' rock home. The next morning the little boy was sent to get his father's horses. While the boy was hunting for the horses, he was captured by a group of Indians. They killed him and left him scalped in full view of the startled people looking out the window. The little boy was buried near the house in what became the Mires Cemetery.

The P.H. (Paddy) Mires house outside of Christoval on the Toenail Trail. Courtesy of Steven Van Court

W. C. Jones completed a long trip when he made it to Christoval in 1874 with his wife Margaret Curry. W. C. was born in Wales and came to America with his family in the 1860s. He and Margaret married in Wisconsin, had four children and decided to move to Texas. First by train and then by wagon they made it to Ft. Concho. The sutler at the fort, Mr. Milspaugh, loaned them a tent, which they pitched on the South Concho River, just west of the present Gene Jones residence. The Jones family built a picket house and commenced ranching.

In the 1880s DeLong was visiting in San Angelo and met a man named Christopher Columbus (C.C.) Doty who was interested in buying some sheep. Doty came from Barry County, Missouri at the age of twenty-one. He finally settled in the South Concho country with his sheep, but it wasn't long until Doty got in a squabble with a cattleman. This rancher said Doty was on his land, and he must leave. Doty conferred with the Land Commission at Austin and found that the cattle rancher only owned 400 acres. The cattleman threatened another sheepman, and Doty interceded by informing the rancher that he knew how much land he actually owned. He said, "If you cause me and my friend any more trouble, we will turn 50,000 sheep loose on your land." Suddenly the cattleman became very friendly.

Sheep were very successful in the Concho Valley until the big crash of 1883-84. At that time, Doty sold out and ranched awhile in Fannin and San Saba counties. The Concho country soon lured Doty back. He worked for a ranch foreman, saved his money and established a store and post office on the South Concho. This location was about three miles north of the present location of Christoval. Doty needed to name the town so he sent in "Alice," but Texas already had a town by that name. Doty sent in the Spanish name for Christopher, which is "Christobal." Authorities couldn't read his writing and changed it to "Christoval."

By 1874, schools began to crop up where just a few families lived near each other. The south side of the Concho River, near present Christoval, was the site of one school in 1874. Further north on the DeLong and Alsop ranches were two more schools. The Loftin School was on Toe Nail Trail. Years ago someone asked a citizen of Christoval why they named the road to Menard the "Toe Nail Trail." The person supposedly

C.C. Doty and his daughter. Courtesy of Billie Marie Van Court

replied, "You have to hold on by your toenails to scratch a living out of this land."

Doty kept the post office and store until a fire wiped it out in the late 1880s. The town of Christoval began to build in its present location after the disaster took place. Doty left Christoval and Uncle Johnny Jones became the postmaster until he was killed by robbers attempting to holdup the post office. In its new location, Christoval began to take on the shape of a real town. The Holland family came in 1879, and they later built the Grove Hotel. The year 1882 saw the W.S. Crawfords and D.Q.

McCartys come into the valley from California. Mr. Crawford built a general mercantile store, which he operated for twenty-five years. Seventeen of those years, he had the post office in the corner of his store.

The town really began to grow in the 1880s. More people came to live there, and the first church formed was a Cumberland Presbyterian Church, where everybody of all denominations worshipped together. In 1891 W. C. Jones gave the land for the church. Men who helped build the church included S. H. Shipley, W. C. Jones, D. Q. McCarty, J. C. Cochran and C.C. Doty. Soon the congregation grew to include about fifty people attending with different protestant preachers taking turns at the pulpit.

Robert Holland tells a funny incident which happened at a Christmas Eve celebration in the Presbyterian Church. He was sitting by Tom, Mike and Orland Sims when Santa Claus came in the front door. Mike said, "I wonder who that is?" Robert said he didn't know, so Mike decided to find out. He struck a match and threw it on Santa's cotton beard. Santa ran to the nearest door. When the fire was put out, the Sims boys discovered that Santa was their Dad.

The 1880s marked not only the forming of a church, but also the start of the South Concho Irrigation Co. Sam DeLong was President and pushed the building of a dam across the river and the creation of three miles of ditches. This irrigation system was longer than the private one that the DeLongs had built several years earlier. Local men helped, but the project would never have been finished if it hadn't been for the soldiers at Fort

Concho. They grabbed shovels and helped to make the ditches a reality. Even with their help, the project took ten years to complete.

Up until the early 1890s, the road from Ben Ficklin to Christoval hugged the South Concho River. However at this time, it was moved away from the river and set in its present location. The new road was widened and fenced because more farmers were coming to the valley. The rancher's livestock had to be separated from the green fields along the river.

Highway departments didn't exist at this time, so each man in the county had to work so many days to repair the roads or he could pay an equal amount in money so repairs could be made. By 1900 the new road was used by Rev. Atkinson's stage, which passed through Christoval.

Newcomers to the Concho country in the early 1900s included two men who loved horses: Lee Williams and William Anson.

Lee's entrance into this country must have turned some heads. Where other ranchers brought herds of cattle, Lee brought 2,200 fine German Coach horses. Now remember this was 1900 and the automobile had made its entrance into the more populated cities. But the horses were very important at this time to many people. Lee settled on four sections of land south of Christoval and raised 1,200 colts annually. There must have been a good market for horses at this time.

In 1902 William A. Anson bought the Head of the River Ranch from the Berrendo Livestock Co. for $3.65 an acre. The

Tankersley family who settled this area earlier had been gone from this ranch for some time. They now ranched along Spring Creek and the Middle Concho. Billy Anson, the new owner, was an Englishmen who became an American citizen in 1896. He served the United States as a Captain in World War I. Anson went from riding horses in battle to riding them to play polo. He traveled in elite circles as he played across the United States.

A story is told about Anson taking his horses to New York to compete in a polo match. He brought some of his cowboy friends to ride in the match. Once the competition started, it didn't take long for the referee to see that the Texans played a different version of polo than the New Yorkers did. The Texans played rough, so they were permanently band from the game. Anson didn't lose at everything he did in New York, though. On one of his trips to New York, he fell in love with Louise Van Wagenen, an accomplished actress. They were eventually married in 1917.

Meanwhile back at the ranch, Anson had to have help with his horses because he was breeding quarter horses as well as thoroughbreds. He employed ten or twelve cowboys most of the time. Some of his foremen were Sid Martin, Dennis Hayes, P.F. Petsch and Lehman Walters.

One of his foremen, P.F. Petsch, had a family and Anson hired a governess to teach the Petsch children in 1904: Snoopy, the tomboy, Tilley, a girl, and Harry, a boy. The teacher, Miss Bertha Reed, had a little stone schoolhouse there on the ranch from which she dispensed the three R's: reading, 'riting and 'rithmetic. After hours, she spent a lot of time with the children.

One of Tilley's favorite places to hide was on top of the

Billy Anson settled at the South Concho Springs in 1901 and raised horses. Courtesy of the West Texas Collection, Angelo State Univ., San Angelo, TX

windmill. This amazed the young teacher. They also visited the spring house for butter and milk. She and the children had the chore of carrying these items to the house. Sometimes they were startled by water moccasins in the spring house.

Since Miss Reed was eighteen at the time, she wasn't much older than the children. They all enjoyed horseback riding.

Once they took off to explore the ranch on horseback. Everything was fine until a sandstorm came up and blinded them. They lost their way home. Finally a Mexican cowboy found them and returned them safely to the ranch. Miss Reed married a cowboy, Robert Preston Schneider in 1906. She convinced him that cowboying wasn't a very dependable job so he quit the ranch and became a carpenter.

1906 was remembered in Christoval for its flood. Twenty miles south of Christoval, it rained twenty-six inches on August 6. The water covered large sections of low land, and the rivers met. The Jake Hannon's family lived on the opposite side of Christoval, near Pecan Creek. As it rained, the water lapped at the porch. The parents decided to bundle up the children, put blankets on their heads too keep out the rain and wade through water that was neck deep.

As they left their house, they looked back to see their pots, pans and one side of the house slip into the river. The children were put up on a windmill that sat on a little knoll. They spent the night there. When the water receded, the family made it to Christoval.

By 1911, Christoval had two doctors: Dr. Salmon and Dr. McCord. Apparently they had a difference of opinion about who was seeing whose patients, so when gunshots were heard in town one day, immediately Maggie Williams told her daughter, "That must be Dr. Salmon. He shot Dr. McCord." Sure enough she was right. Dr. Salmon asked the Baptist Church in Christoval to withdraw fellowship from him on June 4, 1911. He was sentenced to fourteen years in the penitentiary. Ill health and a petition with many signatures on it got him released after serving only seven years.

In later years, Christoval was known for its mineral baths. Thomas Jackson Perciful, born in Dublin, Texas in 1882, received his medical education from the Chiropractic School American University Chicago in 1921 and began practicing at Christoval immediately. Mineral wells, one mile north of Christoval, had natural artesian flows at that time, so it was easy to obtain this water, which was high in sulfur. People already had realized the healing power of this flowing water and were using it to help sick people. Jackson and his brother, D. F. Perciful, bought the business in 1926.

The Healthatorium, as it was called, could serve 55 patients a day. They could keep 48 sick people in Christovals' hotels and in rooms provided by the ten cottages owned by the

This photo is an advertisement of Perciful's Bath House in Christoval

Healthatorium. This facility included sixteen acres that were landscaped like a park because it had roads to drive around, places to walk and benches to sit on. As business picked up, the Percifuls hired three more doctors.

This medical group specialized in the treatment of rheumatism, neuritis, stomach, liver and kidney trouble, eczema and all malignant skin diseases. Patients were given mineral water baths and treatments, ostepathic massage, chiropractic adjustments and asceptic treatments.

In the 1950s Dr. F. W. Rawls opened his treatment center in downtown Christoval. He used the mineral water to treat patients who stayed in his Rawls Bath House, which included rooms for the patients. Many people came to his office for treatments while their families enjoyed fishing and swimming in the nearby South Concho River. Dr. Norman Jenkins, who was Dr. Rawls' son-in-law, took up the practice and continued to treat patients until the facility finally closed. When the doors closed on the Rawls Bath House, much of the equipment to treat such patients was later donated to the Christoval Museum. The bathtubs that held the mineral water were actually made of concrete; they looked very much like a water trough for cattle. No other material could withstand the effects of the sulfur.   As I had a chance to witness the old equipment used on patients, I frankly decided the Bath House was actually a torture chamber. They used shock treatments and their version of colonoscopy equipment looked like it would be very painful for the patient.

However, as I turn to more pleasant topics, I think of the many times that families enjoyed the Baptist Encampment that was held in Christoval. The beautiful banks of the river, lined with shady pecan trees, was the location of the first Christoval Baptist Encampment held in 1911. The camp started with the purchase of 5 acres on the south side of the river near the present City Park. Families put clothes, bedrolls and food in their wagons, drove to Christoval and camped on the river for a week. Each family had their own campfire where three meals a day were prepared. Many people brought a tent to sleep in and as a place to hang their clothes, as well as change them.

Families often camped at the Christoval Baptist Encampment from 1911 until 1932. Courtesy of the West Texas Collection, Angelo State University

A large permanent tabernacle held more than a thousand people the summer of 1916. By 1921, the camp included three two-storied dormitories near the river. The best-known Baptist ministers of Texas came to preach their heart out every summer.

Crowds of five or six thousand people were recorded at the encampment by 1922. A young man named Grady Hill, later a newspaper correspondent, printed a newspaper that told about the successful encampment. All seemed to be fine for the camp until the crash of 1929 affected everybody's' pocket book. The Christoval Baptist Encampment couldn't pay their bills, so the camp closed in 1932.

While this encampment existed, other groups used their facilities to have meetings on the South Concho. According to a 1927 copy of the *San Angelo Standard Times*, the Sixth Annual Texas Artist's Camp opened on the South Concho River. Sixty-two people came the previous year, so the directors of the event were hopeful they would have even more painters this year. Instructors were Will H. Stevens of the Newcomb Art School of New Orleans and Xavier Gonzales of the San Antonio Art School. The public could view the paintings done during the Texas Artist Camp Sunday, July 24, 1927.

During this time, Christoval had one general store on the east side of main street. It was an important stop because it also contained the post office. The drugstore had a soda fountain that was visited by all, and a pharmacist who could cook up almost any prescription from his huge books. There was one doctor in town and he owned the only automobile in town, a Model T Ford. The only way you could start it was by the use of a crank. The doctor always tried to get somebody else to crank his car, partly because it was hard to do and sometimes you broke an arm trying to crank. Maybe the doctor needed more patients. Meanwhile other settlements were cropping up on

Dove Creek and Spring Creek at the same time as the community of Christoval emerged.

Picture of a group of artists who took part in the art camp on the South Concho at Christoval. Courtesy of Christoval Museum.

Chapter 3 – Knickerbocker's Ruckus

During the 1860s, cavalrymen ventured through the Dove Creek region, but they saw few settlers along the rivers or draws. The soldiers were usually chasing Indians, but they did see R. F. Tankersley. His cattle ranged from the South Concho River to Dove Creek. At this time the area had no fences, so it was open range separated only by rivers. A few German settlers were found in the draws.

Some of the first inhabitants of the Dove Creek area were the Baze brothers. Williams Benjamin Baze and wife Jane moved from Missouri to central Texas, probably near Lampasas County in the 1850s. They had four sons: Michael Polk, Dewey Franklin, William Thomas and Abednego Peter.

Each of the Baze sons explored Texas before arriving at Dove Creek. Polk drove cattle for John Chisum on his drives out of state. He also hunted buffalo near the head of Dove Creek and the Concho River. Pete Baze served as a Confederate soldier in the Second Brigade of Texas. He turned to law enforcement and served as Sheriff of Lampasas County in 1866 and Justice of the Peace in Tom Green County in 1876.

Tom Baze was in the Ben Ficklin community, also part of Tom Green County, at the same time. Proof of this is that his and Cerena May Ellis' marriage license issued in 1878 was one of only two such known licenses issued from that town. Ben Ficklin was washed away a short time later, in 1882.

In 1875 the four Baze brothers bought land north of Dove Creek from Sam Maverick for 870 gold dollars. Soon a large, two-storied house was built by Pete Baze, and he put chimneys on each end. Pete helped settle the Baze community by donating an acre for the Baze Cemetery and another acre in 1877 for a school. The cemetery had a fence around it with a metal entrance, "Baze Cemetery," on an arch above. It still stands at this time.

Visitors at the Baze Cemetery during its receiving a Texas Historical Marker. Author's photo

The Baze schoolhouse soon became the hub of community affairs. Dimensions of 30 feet by 40 feet allowed room for a stage at one end of the school. Large windows brought in plenty of light. "The Adobe School," complete with shingled roof and pine floors, was the logical place for social events, elections and school functions. Early teachers who taught at the Baze School included Willie Landrum, a Church of Christ minister, and Miss Matt Ryan.

The Baze brothers also built a gravity flow irrigation system in 1877. Their dam was about one mile southwest of the present Dove Creek bridge that brings travelers to Knickerbocker from the west. Most of the irrigated land was northwest of the bridge toward the Baze Community. At one time this bridge was called the Red Bridge. The present Lewis Runion Development, west of Dove Creek, included most of this farming acreage. The Bismarck Farm project, east of the city of San Angelo, was completed in 1868, so the Baze Ditch was the second irrigation system in the county.

In May of 1877, Joseph Tweedy, a 28-year-old man, came to Fort Concho to scout for a new sheep ranch. His parents had migrated from Scotland to New York, and this sheepherder had already found a flock of sheep at Fort Clark that he liked. He was visiting the Concho country to find grazing land that he could buy. In a letter written home from Fort Concho, he said, "Have seen some desirable country on the Concho and tributary streams West of here – which we might be able to get."

Later in 1877 Joseph Tweedy and his partners, E. Morgan Grinnell, Lawrence Grinnell and J. Barlow Reynolds drove 1, 200 Mexican ewes to their new home on Dove Creek. They were the first sheep to come into the valley. These four men had leased or bought 20,000 acres of land. Their headquarters were on the east side of Dove Creek, which was about a half mile from the present town and about one mile from the Baze Community.

When the four partners built their headquarters, it included two frame houses, a bunkhouse and ranch kitchen and a two-story store. The frame houses were one-storied with ample porch space. These buildings were called the Knickerbocker Ranch Headquarters. How the men came up with the "Knickerbocker" name was interesting.

Tweedy Headquarters with residence to the left and two-storied store on the right. Courtesy of West Texas Collection at Angelo State Univ. at San Angelo.

The Grinnell brothers said that they were identifying the place by the name to honor their famous uncle, Washington Irving. He was often called the "father of American literature," but the average reader doesn't know his "other" name. Irving used a pseudonym name as the author of some of his writings.

In 1809 when he wrote *History of New York,* he used his other name, Diedrick Knickerbocker.

Soon other families came to Knickerbocker also. Carl Joseph Schmidt migrated to this area in 1883 from Bexar County. He did cowboy work on the local ranches, including Berry Ketchum's ranch, which was several miles east of the Knickerbocker townsite.

W. F. Holt helped the Army drive livestock from California to Fort Concho in the late 1870s. While at the fort, he met a buffalo hunter named Henry Moses Johnson. This fellow furnished the soldiers with meat and hides. W. F. got to know Johnson and discovered that he had a pretty daughter named Sallie. In March of 1886, W. F. Holt married Sallie, and they settled in Knickerbocker. At that residence, he was Justice of the Peace and was the first Sunday School superintendent at the local church. Later Mr. Holt became judge of Tom Green County. He was known as a historian, postmaster, road superintendent and religious worker. These were relatively mild activities compared to his early escapades.

W. F. Holt was sent to bring in the cows one day at his first home in Baltimore, Maryland. W. F. was sixteen that year of 1866. Life was so tame that he decided to run away. He hid in a ship that was in port at the time. Once the ship left port, Holt had many adventures including shipwrecks. In the South Sea Islands, he was captured by natives, and a pot was prepared to boil him alive, but he was saved from death by the tribal queen. He lived to tell the tale and come to Texas.

S. D. Arthur came to Knickerbocker in 1887 from Marlin, Texas. Stephen Dexter, S. D., brought one hundred longhorn cattle with him on the trail. He was tired of planting cotton in his other home, but he brought cotton seed along to feed his cows on the trail. Some seed was left over after his first winter, so he decided to plant a little to see if it would grow in this new place. 1888 proved to be a good cotton year in Knickerbocker, and Arthur's first bales were hauled to a gin in Coleman. This was a long trip by wagon. It wasn't until 1894 that Arthur built a water-powered gin on the west side of Dove Creek near the present highway bridge.

Oran H. Atkins and wife, Martha, moved to Knickerbocker in 1881. Their son, John Atkins, was born earlier in 1866 at Kickapoo Springs, some miles southeast of Fort Concho. Even so, he was considered the first white child born in this area.

Sheep coming to Knickerbocker was certainly noticed by one cattle rancher, Richard Tankersley. He asked Joseph Tweedy, "Why did you want to bring sheep into this area?

Joseph replied, "I don't know why not?" Surprisingly the two men never fought over grassland for their animals. There seemed to be enough grazing for both.

The next several years were bad for the sheepmen, and in 1884, the four men: two Grinnells, Reynolds, and Tweedy decided to dissolve their partnership. Their extended credit was demanding $4,000 in interest annually in 1883. That was a lot of money at that time.

Morgan Grinnell had married Sallie J. Stone in 1881 in New York. Joseph Tweedy had also returned east to marry Elizabeth Mellick the same year. When the ranching partnership dissolved, Morgan and his bride returned to New York. Lawrence Grinnell left Knickerbocker and died in New York in 1881. Reynolds departed to Omaha, so this left only Joseph Tweedy and his new bride to continue ranching along Dove Creek. Joseph "hung tight" to his land through the lean years as well as the good ones. His descendents still ranch part of Joseph's ranch at this time.

Although some people left Knickerbocker, others were moving into the village beside the Dove Creek waters. During the 1880s, brothers Honesimo and Adriano Jacques with their families came to the Dove Creek area from Ben Ficklin where the Flood of 1882 washed everything away. The Jacques family's trek to this country was long however and it began in Europe.

About 1800 Thomas Jacques was born in Spain or in France, his descendants weren't sure. He migrated to Chihuahua, Mexico in 1820 and married Guadalupe Romero. They and their children, Josefa, Trinidad, Honesimo, Adriano, and Jesus Jose, lived through turbulent times in southern Chichuachua. The Apaches and the Comanches were on the warpath in that region as well as invading General Doniphan of the Mexican-American War. Following this upheaval came economic depression, drought and a revolution between the liberals and the conservatives in 1862 – 1868.

Finally the Jacques family had enough strife, so they decided to leave Mexico and travel to Fort Stockton by wagon. This trip continued until Thomas and his three sons settled near Ben Ficklin. Thomas signed the petition to form Tom Green County in 1872.

By 1886 Honesimo, son of Thomas Jacques, and his wife Salome Rodriquez moved to Knickerbocker. Salome brought an interesting heritage with her. Her father, Jose Rodriquez was an Indian scout, and her mother was thought to have been part Indian. Salome knew which plants were edible and how to make pottery from the clay found along the riverbanks. She was listed on the census as midwife and as a schoolteacher. Honesimo and Salome enjoyed music in their home. The boys played instruments and the girls had pretty singing voices.

Another interesting lady of Knickerbocker was Alvina Venegas. In 1879 she was only thirteen, but she knew she wanted to leave her home in Shafter, Texas. A fifteen-year old boy agreed to marry her and take her to the community of Ben Ficklin. She agreed to go with him, and after the wedding, the two teenagers headed to Ben Ficklin along with her parents. Alvina's husband was shot when he chased a run-away horse on another man's pasture, so Alvina became a very young widow. Although the loss of Alvina's husband was sad, she along with her family decided to continue their long journey northeastward. They finally came to the Ben Ficklin and Knickerbocker area.

Alvina married Anselmo Flores in 1882, and they had the following children: Dolores, Pilar and Basilo. Her husband took a trip to New Mexico, presumably to check on his family's sheep ranch. Anselmo made this trip without his wife. As the story goes, Anselmo was struck with amnesia and didn't come back home to Knickerbocker.

Soon Alvinia found husband number three: one man named Jesus Delgado. Alvinia and Jesus married in 1890, but he was killed in a fight in a Sonora barroom, so she was on her own again. Alvinia seemed to know how to survive even when she was dealt much hardship.

She worked at several jobs at the same time. Alvinia was a housekeeper for the Tweedy and the Prescott family. She also raised domestic animals and a vegetable garden. This woman purchased land and eventually built a large house on it. She took in renters to supplement her income. She also helped Dr. Boyd Cornick with laundry in his Sanatorium in Knickerbocker.

Seems as though Alvinia's second husband, Anselmo, came out of his amnesia and heard that his wife was going to marry a young man, Fredrico Jacques. Since he now remembered where Alvinia lived, Anselmo brought his new family on the long trip from New Mexico all the way to Knickerbocker. After the arrival of the forgetful husband, Alvinia rounded up her children and had a picture taken of them along with the brood that came with Anselmo. The long lost husband didn't live many days after this unusual reunion. After his death, Alvinia married Fredrico, but she soon realized she wanted a divorce from him. The same day that the divorce was final, she married Filomeno Morales.

Changes not quite as drastic as Alvinia's life continued to take place in the little community as well as in people's lives. The town of Knickerbocker began to develop as mail and stage lines materialized. In 1881 a mail route began from South Concho to the head of Spring Creek, which would pass through Knickerbocker. Also a stage line was to travel from San Angelo to Knickerbocker to Sherwood to Big Lake and on to Natural Wells.

Arrangements for these stops had to be made and horses had to be kept in nearby pens for the stages that came through. The stage driver usually changed horses about every 20 miles. At Knickerbocker they were fed and penned near the old red bridge on Dove Creek, which was near the present bridge in use. The first post office was at the Baze Community. However, the Tweedys wanted it at their store. They petitioned for the post office to be moved, and so it began to be housed in a corner of the red painted Grinnell, Tweedy and Reynolds Mercantile Store.

Knickerbocker had grown at this location. It had two saloons, a combination blacksmith-undertaker shop, three stores, two hotels, stage line stables and a Tuberculosis Sanatorium. Two men were involved in the Sanatorium business.

One person was Dr. Boyd Cornick, who came to this area to find dry clean air that would help his own tuberculosis symptoms in 1900. Although he bought a farm in Knickerbocker, Cornick built his home in San Angelo on Main Street the following year. Dr. Cornick believed in a high-protein diet, hygiene, rest, mild exercise and sleeping in the open air. By 1930 he had thirty houses at Cornick Bungalows, where he treated tuberculosis patients and used his regime.

Another small convalescent center for tuberculosis was built by Mr. Blanchard, who was a former San Angelo postmaster. He bought land from Joseph Tweedy on the side of the large hill near Knickerhbocker and built three or four rooms. He only had one patient, so after a few years his clinic closed its doors, and the land went back to Tweedy.

While Blanchard's idea failed, Cornick's bungalows didn't. Dr. Cornick wrote the State's first sanitary code and was instrumental in the building of the Tuberculosis Sanitorium at Carlsbad.

The blacksmith shop owned by George and Fred Davis in Knickerbocker was unique. The bottom floor was a blacksmith shop and the top floor was where they kept the coffins. On the top of the blacksmith shop was a windmill with a little wooden man on the wheel. The man had a hammer in his hand, and as the wheel turned, the hammer struck the anvil.

The Tweedys now had competition in retail since Willie Prescott and Tom Hardin also owned stores in Knickerbocker. Prescott had a hotel as well as did Mrs. Henry Johnson. She also had a café to feed hungry travelers. Knickerhocker was in good shape as far as retail goes, but they had no school, church or cemetery. They had to depend on the Baze settlement for these.

With so many new people coming to Knickerbocker to live, the community leaders realized they couldn't get enough water at their present location. Shallow, hand dug wells weren't efficient, so they decided to move the town about a mile south, which is its present location. In 1889 buildings such as the Tweedy Store, Prescott Store and Blacksmith Shop were moved to the present town site. Joseph Tweedy donated land for a church, and the community donated money to buy the lumber. The building materials were hauled from Round Rock, Texas by S. D. Arthur and the community helped to build the church.

The small Protestant church was heated by a wood-burning stove in the middle of the room. The bell was mounted on the top of the red plank church. It sounded the start of the worship services and was used when funeral services were held. The bell rang once for each year of the deceased's life.

Summertime saw church held in a different setting: a brush arbor. This structure was made with upright poles along the sides, which held up the brush piles on top for shade. Sawdust was sprinkled in the aisles to keep down the dust. When a new convert joined the church, they called it "Hitting the sawdust trail."

A place for the Catholics to worship was needed also. In 1888 only a small Catholic mission was present on the Tweedy farm and documents show that year a wedding took place in the little sanctuary. Land for a proper Catholic church of Knickerbocker was purchased in 1889. The first building was made in 1908. A much larger building was purchased from Goodfellow Air Base in 1947 and moved to Knickerbocker. The present site of the Catholic church is where both early structures were located.

When the citizens of Knickerbocker weren't going to church activities, they had other meetings to keep their social life busy. After the old Tweedy store was moved to its new location, the Woodsmen of the World, a man's lodge, met on its second floor. The men of the community also had the Masons meetings to attend. Mrs. Tweedy organized the King's Daughters, an organization for the women. The second floor of the Prescott Store was where the dances were held.

The stage line brought people and the mail to the little town on Dove Creek. When the driver neared Knickerbocker, he blew his horn so the stable hand could get the new team ready. A minute or two later, the crowd gathered around the Jack Douglas stables could see the hack coming. This stage had a white top and two or three seats. It really looked like a wagon with seats. The four-horse hitch had the two lead horses in front, and the two others hitched to the tongue of the wagon.

When the driver stopped, the passengers quickly jumped out for a drink from the common gourd dipper. While the mail was whisked away to the post office, the stable hands were switching the horses. By the time the four fresh mounts were ready to roll, the driver had hollered "All aboard," and a cloud of dust indicated that the stage was on its way to Sherwood.

Knickerbocker had its own gun play at Brown's Saloon in 1897. Sam and Joe Moore began the commotion by firing shots over Tom Hardin's house after dark. Tom thought the bullets came from the nearby saloon, so he entered the establishment and told all in earshot that they'd better quit shooting at his house.

Dave Atkins was a part of the crowd and obviously didn't like Tom's speech. He fired and killed the agitated man on the spot. Brown's Saloon was just south of the present Community Church. Tom Hardin built a house south of this saloon, and this dwelling still stands today. It is known as the Etheridge house.

After this episode, Dave was on the run for many years. According to a manuscript he dictated to his niece, he found lots of places to hide in the Knickerbocker area. He stayed in the Charlie Beck Hollar and in the Preacher Thicket when he was ducking the law. Both places were near Knickerbocker. Dave also rode with a local outlaw, Black Jack Ketchum, some of the time.

Dave left the country for South America before the law got him. Only when he returned to Knickerbocker, was he put in prison for the Hardin murder. After his release, he returned to Knickerbocker again to live until his mental health deteriorated. When he was found eating his own horse, which he had shot, Dave was committed to the Wichita Falls State hospital for the Insane.

Several interesting hiding places were west of Knickerbocker and Dave Atkins occupied them all at one time or another. Charlie Beck Hollow was believed to be on the west end of the Tweedy ranch where the draw flows out of the Winterbottom ranch. The upper end of Dove Creek also had a thicket called Boot-legger Thicket. Evidence that moonshine was made here could be found a long time after prohibition was instigated. The metal distillation containers, along with metal tubing, was found there.

White Lightning was often made closer to home. According to Arthur Franco, most of the alcohol he remembered seeing as a boy was made nearby. He said, "Hiding it was the trick." Arthur explained that the bottles of booze were put in a basket and lowered into a well. There it was hidden and kept cool.

In the early years of Knickerbocker, its stores didn't always have enough coins to make the correct change due a customer. Like other towns, they produced tokens to give in place of coins. Tokens were common tender from the 1880s until the time of prohibition. Although saloons were most well known as businesses that gave tokens, other businesses did this also. A shopper could receive tokens from a general store, groceries, department stores, taverns and barbers. Tokens often were stamped with a value of 5 cents, ten cents, or 12 and a half cents, also called two bits.

At this time it was hard to keep enough change because businessmen weren't close to a big bank. Saloon names were usually printed on their tokens, and most of the citizens knew that a saloon token was good for a "smile," a small whiskey. Tokens were made of brass or aluminum

Most of the Knickerbocker citizens were more interested in educating their offspring rather than finding a killer or paying for whiskey. By 1889 a frame schoolhouse was built on the present school site. A red brick school was built to replace it in the 1930s and still stands as the Knickerbocker Community Center.

Activity related to community schools was very important in 1902. A columnist writing from Knickerbocker to the *San Angelo Standard Times* often discussed education in the column "Knick Knacks," which was about life in Knickerbocker. Separate from the regular public schools, instruction could be held in subjects such as "writing." Mr. McGee enrolled sixty Knickerbocker pupils in writing January 29, 1902, and Walter Johnson taught a writing school in Knickerbocker later in March of the same year.

Dr. Boyd Conick lived near the Baze Community in 1890. He found that the Hispanic children were banned from the public schools, so he pushed for them to have a school. The first Mexican school was built in 1896. This structure was built east of the highway, directly across the street from Romulo Morale's house. It continued as a school until 1948 when its students combined with the white public school. Miss Beck was the first teacher of the Spanish school. When she married, she could no longer teach because only single women were allowed to be employed by schools. Gilberto Cruz came to Knickerbocker with the title of "professor" and taught in the Mexican School. At a later time, Lucille Duncan taught in the school for many years.

Faculty from several schools often banned together to have teacher meetings. Teachers from Tom Green and Irion

Dr. Boyd Cornick developed a tuberculosis Sanatorium and helped build a Spanish school in Knickerbocker. Courtesy of the West Texas Collection, Angelo State Univ.

counties attended a Teacher's Institute, which was held in Knickerbocker January 29, 1902. One of the speakers at the institute was Gilberto Cruz. He presented a paper on "The Importance of Teaching Spanish in Our Schools." Gilberto's life ended with a sudden illness in May of that same year. His widow, Guillermita, taught in his place for several years.

Berry Ketchum ranched both in Knickerbocker and on the Pecos. He was an upright citizen, quite different from his younger brothers, Tom and Sam. They hit the outlaw trail whereas Berry seemed to stay within the law. The older Ketchum brother tried to learn what was new in ranching. Berry Ketchum and Frank Parker went to the Cattlemen's Convention in March of 1902 according to a statement in the *San Angelo Standard Times*.

Many of the people coming into Knickerbocker had particular skills. Some had many such as Barnabe Martinez who came with his bride, Maria Jordan, in 1879. Barnabe wore many different hats. He was a carpenter, stonemason and tailor. He made clothes for his family as well as for the public. After living on the Tweedy farm and working, he built his family a house in Knickerbocker. When he wasn't building a house, he was building coffins or chiseling tombstones. Barnabe made a tombstone for his father-in-law, "Ysidoro Jordan and for himself. They are in the Catholic Cemetery. Barnabe felt that education was important for his children. When Knickerbocker schools wouldn't integrate the Mexican children, he moved to San Angelo each September so his children could go to school there.

Barnabe Martinez , 1850 – 1930, early Knickerbocker settler.
Courtesy of Paul Martinez.

While Knickerbocker was developing on Dove Creek, another community called Sherwood was appearing due west, about twelve miles as the crow flies.

A stagecoach leaving the Concho Mail Station near Fort Concho. Stagecoaches traveled from Fort Concho to Knickerbocker and over the hill westward to Sherwood. Courtesy of the West Texas Collection at Angelo state University.

Chapter 4 – Sherwood's Ruckus

The future location of Irion County along the banks of Spring Creek and Middle Concho was a wild country in 1865. Cavalry chasing Indians in that area described its only inhabitants as being buffalo, wolves, prairie dogs and Indians. No roads were visible; only cow trails could be used. The few homes scattered along the river were either made of picket or were dugouts.

Even so, when Charley and William Lackey reined in their horses and viewed the fertile land along Spring Creek in 1878, it must have reminded them of their home in Kentucky. The river was lined with shady pecan and live oak trees. Soon they built a house of picket and covered it with canvas. William had probably seen Spring Creek when he was involved in the Dove Creek Massacre some thirteen years before this trip. But he probably didn't get this far west on his military rendezvous. The Lackey's next order of business was to start farming, so they set up an irrigation system to water vegetables from Spring Creek. The Lackeys dug ditches and made a rock and log dam.

The irrigation system soon attracted other families to Spring Creek. A little town of Sherwood began to develop on the southeast side of the river about twenty-five miles southwest of San Angelo. But in 1882 a terrible flood pushed water out of the river and onto the little town. In Sherwood it destroyed dams, ditches, people's homes and killed their livestock. M. E. Merrill tied his young son up in a sheet and placed him in a big pecan

Children in front of a picket house similar to the one the Lackeys built in Sherwood. Courtesy of West Texas Collection, Angelo State Univ.

tree so the swirling floodwaters wouldn't wash him away. Merrill went to look for the rest of his family and didn't check on the boy for 24 hours. His wife and other children were found dead, but his son remained a safe, but tired boy. Across the road from the Sherwood Cemetery, there stands today a lone metal fence enclosing graves of this family.

After the flood, the town of Sherwood was rebuilt further southeast away from the water. The dam was reconstructed so irrigation could continue and the cooperating group of farmers called themselves the Upper Ditch Company. As the town enlarged, the need for farmers to grow more food increased. In 1886 a reporter from the *San Angelo Standard Times* wrote to his readers that Sherwood was "quite a garden of Eden." One could see melons, cabbages, turnips, tomatoes and sweet potatoes growing. Sherwood had its own canning factory, which turned out as many as 500 cans of vegetables a day in 1889.

Work wasn't scheduled for every day. On holidays, such as the Fourth of July, people got together from all three communities: Christoval, Knickerbocker, and Sherwood. This national holiday was spent with a picnic at the head of Dove Creek in 1885. The caterers were from the Dove Creek area, and after eating, they began to dance about 2 p.m. The festivities lasted until the wee hours of the next day. People present were Mr. Hilloman and wife, the hosts; Mr. William Smith of the Six Ranch; Mr. W. C. Jones and family of the South Concho; Col. B. W. Dozier and Miss Mert Merrill and others from Sherwood.

Probably the earliest community in present Irion County wasn't Sherwood at all. Files at Fort Concho National Historic Landmark indicate there existed a Camp Charlotte at two different locations west of Sherwood on Kiowa Creek. It was mentioned as early as 1848. This fort was said to be on the Middle Concho River below the mouth of Kiowa Creek. Since the Butterfield Stage Line operated the Overland Mail through there from 1857 to 1869, it served as a post office from 1885 to 1899. Old timers remember the frame post office in the newer location of Camp Charlotte. This place was about one mile east of the original Camp Charlotte. The original camp was a stockade 190 feet long and 115 feet wide. The stable was inside the fort and measured 75 by 150 feet.

SCENE ON S RANCH, AT MOUTH OF KIOWA CREEK, 1886

LEE MINOR, Ranch Boss
G. W. TANKERSLY
W. J. CARSON
UNCLE JACK COX

Many old-timers will recognize this picture on the S ranch, taken at a point about 400 yards south of old Camp Charlotte. We give name of our grand old ranch boss, Lee Minor

This scene with local cowboys was situated 400 yards south of old Camp Charlotte on Kiowa Creek. Courtesy of West Texas Collection, Angelo State University.

Officers' quarters and the guardhouse were outside the east main gate. Troopers slept in their tents inside the fort. Since they were infantry, these soldiers could do little to stop the Indians who drove off livestock from the fort in 1874. In 1882 Company F of the 16th Infantry of Fort Concho were instructed to move to Camp Charlotte. If this description of the fort gives you the impression it was made of some strong material like rocks, think again. Its picket walls were made of tree limbs and mud.

On December 27, 1867, Capt. G. G. Hunt, 4th U.S. Cavalry Commander of Camp Heath wrote a letter to his superior reporting a scouting trip near Camp Charlotte. The officer had heard that civilians had been murdered by Indians near the Overland Stage crossing of the Concho River. On December 21,

1867, they found four bodies in a wash in the bank of a stream. Another body was found about fifty paces away from the water.

The murdered men were brothers: James and John Ketchum, Robert Correpossa, William Truman and Thomas Donnell. James Ketchum had sold some cattle in New Mexico and was returning to his home in San Saba. James Ketchum's body showed signs of torture, charred and blackened spots. His money was scattered all about. Price Cooper from San Saba, one of the soldiers at the scene, took the money to give it to James' relatives on his next trip to San Saba.

Hunt followed the Indian trail with seven of his men but found only smoldering campfires left by a large band of Indians. He had seven days of rations and needed to travel 130 miles to return his troops to Fort Hatch (Fort Concho.)

The question comes up as to whether this James Ketchum was kin to Black Jack Ketchum, the outlaw from Knickerbocker. The 1860 Census of Texas shows John Ketchum, a thirty-four year old male and his family living in San Saba County at the same time Green B. Ketchum was there.

Green and Constance Ketchum were the parents of Black Jack and Sam Ketchum who later hit the outlaw trail. Green was thirty-eight years old in 1860. He was listed as being born in Alabama and his wife was born in Illinois. James Ketchum was born in Illinois, so one would believe there was a family connection.

When Indian raids decreased, the official decree came from Austin in April of 1889 that a county called Irion was to be carved out of the large existing Tom Green County. Sherwood would be the new county seat. By July a stone contractor W. A. McKnight was ready to build the small two-story courthouse, that would act as the jail, but contain several rooms for offices. People were quite interested when the steel cages came by freight and were placed in the upstairs area to complete the jail. Nearly 400 inhabitants formed a community now with 2 general stores, 3 livery stables, 2 hotels and other businesses. They had 2 private schools, one run by Prof. Brown and one by Mrs. Sublett and together taught 120 pupils.

Sherwood citizens used the small jailhouse to carry out their county business until plans were finalized for a bigger courthouse. This new building was made of local queried limestone. It included four offices on the first floor with halls opening to outside doors in the center of each side of the building. The second floor included two more offices and a large courtroom. The new structure was completed in 1901.

The community enjoyed the large room on the second floor of the courthouse. Sometime they had dances, teacher's institutes or summer socials in the ample space. A wooden fence prevented livestock from grazing the courthouse lawn.

A stage line served Sherwood by coming from Ozona to Sherwood and on to San Angelo. One man who drove this line was Walter Dunlap. Ross McSwain interviewed Walter about his stage driving.

The Sherwood Courthouse was completed about 1901 and still stands today. Author's collection.

Walter said he could make the tip from Ozona a lot quicker than many drivers because he tied the reins to his stage, jumped off, ran to open the gates and jumped back on. Once he saw the Ketchum gang as he was driving through the country, but they didn't bother him.

As the town grew, so did the farming. In August of 1889, William Lackey was apologetic that his cotton was making only a bale and a half to the acre. Since cotton was successful, several men including an engineer named H. P. Howe, decided to build a cotton gin in the Sherwood area. In 1903 the gin company was organized with Mabry J. Norrell as president, H. P. Howe as operator and manager, and stockholders Fayette Tankersley, Jeff St. Clair and W. W. Carson.

They were able to buy a steam engine in Coleman from Will H. Bell and haul it to San Angelo in 1903. After unloading it from the train, the engine was headed toward Sherwood.

Mr. Howe, his son Earl and W. K. Beaty were in San Angelo to claim the engine. The boiler was filled, a fire made in the bin and when it built up enough pressure, the trip began. The three men kept it burning as it traveled the 25 miles from San Angelo to Sherwood. The journey required two days. As the steam engine arrived in the little community, teachers turned school out so the kids could see the "hissing monster" move down the main street of Sherwood.

Ranching competed with the farming as a very successful livelihood at this time. A Californian by the name of John Arden brought in the first sheep in the area in 1884. Sheepmen were often called "flockmasters" in this area. Their concerns were the price of the wool and illnesses that the sheep had. Scabies had infected the sheep by 1891. The sick sheep had rough, mangy skin. The scaby outbreak was so bad that William Lackey was designated sheep inspector of Irion County. He had several deputies who he called "practical sheepmen." They went through the flocks and isolated the sick sheep. Of course flockmasters hated to see them coming because once the sick sheep were found, they were killed. On the first assessed valuation of Irion County taxes in 1889, sheep in the county were numbered as 29,000 and cattle were 34,000.

The first white family to settle in this area as a cattleman was Fayette Tankersley's family. At the age of 17 in 1886, he helped his father, R. F. Tankersley, drive longhorn steers to Fort Worth. Fayette's pay for the drive was 50 heifers and this livestock was the beginning of his successful ranching career.

By 1904 he was stocking Durham cattle and later switched to registered Hereford cattle.

In 1884 public school land owned by the State of Texas was put up for sale. Fayette bought four sections of this land and strung the first barbed wire around it that the people of this area had probably ever seen. As he continued to buy land, his holdings soon exceeded 20 sections. Tankersley was now ranching in Irion County and managed the 7D Ranch. Another "soon to be" rancher came to this area in 1871.

Philetus Sawyer was a successful lumberman in Oashkosh, Wisconsin. He loaned some money to a Texan, and the man repaid his dept so quickly that Sawyer decided to come to Texas to see what made this person so prosperous. When Sawyer got to Irion County, he began to buy ranch land. From that time until 1920 Sawyer purchased 269 sections. S. E. Sterrett and George Sherwood sold their holdings on the Middle Concho to him in 1884. That one transaction included 10,000 cattle and 8,000 acres of riverfront property. Cattle were brought from San Saba County and placed on the Middle Concho River near Kiowa Creek, not far from Camp Charlotte.

Open range took care of 7D cows right along side of Sawyers' Bar S stock for four years. Finally in 1884, the two ranchers met and set boundaries. Then fences were built. Other men wanted to be successful ranchers, and Sherwood had just the right opportunity for them.

A public land sale was announced. During the final days of March 1903, droves of people headed to the tiny town of Sherwood, Texas by whatever means they had. Some came by train, but they had to get off the train in San Angelo because there wasn't a railroad track from San Angelo to Sherwood. Others rented a hack or rode by horseback. Some would-be-land buyers may have walked. The State of Texas was selling seventy-six sections of school land that resided in Irion County. The public announcement said that people could buy the land for one dollar an acre unless it included riverfront property. In that case, the land was one dollar and a half per acre. If there was land available in Irion County when the County Clerk received your application, you could buy as much as four sections.

This offer sounded like a good deal to many people in 1903 because you only had to pay one fortieth of the purchase price down and you would have forty years to pay it out at 3%. If a cowboy bought two sections for a dollar an acre, he would owe $1,280, but he would only have to pay down $38.40.

There were some limitations, however. Several years before this sale, Texas Land Commissioner John J. Terrell had driven for miles and miles along the fences of recently purchased public land. He saw no improvements or sign of people living on the land. This factor brought about some new rules. Terrell decreed that a person must live on the land for a minimum of three years, be there on the ranch at least six months out of each year and make improvements for the purchase to be valid.

At an earlier time, women had filed so they could buy three sections for themselves. This acreage could be added to the four sections their husband bought for a total of seven sections for one family. A 1900 law repealed this procedure and said women couldn't buy land if their husband had already purchased some because this act gave families unfair advantage over others.

Sherwood was situated remotely twenty-five miles west of San Angelo in West Texas. The train tracks stopped at San Angelo, so determined people who planned to be at the land rush had to find other means for transportation to get to the county seat of Irion County. This problem didn't seem to bother them because a trainload of people from the east entered San Angelo about a week before the event would take place on March 7 in Sherwood.

The land available for sale was part of some existing ranches, which were currently leased by cattlemen and sheepherders. The lease would terminate March 7, 1903, and be offered for sale that morning to the first man filing at 7:30 a.m. at the county courthouse. Part of the available land came from the 06 Ranch leased by Willis Johnson; part was the Ryburn pasture, part was the O9 Ranch, two sections lay in the H. W. Gillis ranch, and two sections were in the Bird and Mertz pasture.

Legislators sensed there might be some little misunderstandings of the laws governing land rushes so far reaching legislature was discussed in the senate chambers some 200 miles away in Austin. Three days before the sale took place, Senator J. W. Hill tried to pass a bill by the Texas Senate to avoid trouble. His proposed bill "prescribed a period of limitation within which any person claiming the right to purchase or lease public free school, state, university or asylum lands heretofore sold or leased to others, shall bring this suit therefore, providing that such suits shall be brought within ninety days after the passage of the act, otherwise title is unassailable."

Seems as though even in 1903 politicians could word a bill where most of us had no idea what it meant. After much discussion, the bill was tabled until March 12, 1903, after the Irion County Land Rush.

The only material passed was a resolution in the house that "authorized the land commissioner to withhold school and asylum lands from sale pending legislation deciding the method of making application to purchase."

But this rule made no difference to the would-be-ranchers who kept coming to Sherwood in spite of legislators. Mr. W. W. Carson, the County Clerk, prepared for the event. He wanted the land purchasers to line up outside the limestone courthouse and file their claims through an open window to his office. To make this effective at 7:30 a.m. on Saturday morning of March 7, he had a chute built. By using the chute, Carson could herd the land seekers in a single line to this window and have no problems, so he thought.

Early Friday morning, nearly twenty-four hours before the Clerk's window would open for business, two men tied themselves to the window so they could be first in line. W. E. Branch, editor of the *Irion County Record,* and Harry Francis, a well-known citizen of the area, tied themselves to the window with ropes and straps. They were two strong, muscular characters, so they thought they had it made. They remained there during the night while other men lined up behind them, about one hundred cowboys in all. March weather could be quite cool at night, but the would-be ranch owners didn't seem to mind the elements. They were going to own ranch land.

Shortly after midnight, in the wee hours of Saturday morning, Clerk Carson decided to slip into his office. However, he didn't realize that H. H. Mitchell was right behind him. Mitchell pushed into Carson's office with a bunch of applications for land. He demanded that Carson file them immediately rather than wait until 7:30 the next morning. Carson told him to leave, but Mitchell kept advancing toward the clerk. Carson reached nearby for a heavy seal on his desk. He used it to take a swipe at the oncoming Mitchell. Instead of hitting the rancher, Carson knocked over a burning lamp.

As the ignited oil spread from the broken lamp, the two men scuffled, and the applications got burned in the fire. Mitchell gave up and both men started to leave. The smoke was so strong that Carson opened an outside window from the top to let the smoke escape through the transom. Another applicant, Frank Allison from nearby Eldorado, was ready with his papers. He flung them in the window and demanded that they be filed. Carson refused his request but did offer to pick them up and give

W. W. Carson, Irion County Clerk who filed the land purchases.
Courtesy of the Irion County Historical Society

them back to Allison. The angry rancher refused to accept them, so his papers remained on the floor during the entire land rush.

As the sun inched over the cedar and oak-dotted hills around Sherwood, the crowd of participants and onlookers increased. The cowboys from the 06 Ranch decided it was time to make their move and gain a place in the line before things started at 7:30. They closed ranks, rushed towards where Branch and Francis were perched on the Clerk's window. They wrestled the two men from their position in the front of the line.

The two men came popping out of the window "like two big overripe apples," described a newspaper reporter. By grabbing the two men's legs, the Sixers pulled them from their lofty perch on the window sill and threw them to the side.

Now the line of applicants had Sixer boys in the front and other local men were forced to take a position at the end. Applications were collected from the friends of the Sixers and handed to the men in front of the line.

All wasn't settled though. Next enters the "outsiders" from other towns. It was their turn to fight, and fight they did. A terrific wrestling match took place. Men would clinch in combat, fall on the ground wrestling and then roll around in the dirt. Shirts were torn, dirty faces were bruised and eyes got puffy, but no one was mortally wounded. The Sixers held their position until all their applications had been filed. Other men got the less desirable land that was left.

The crowd had swelled to about one hundred and fifty before the fun was over. Everybody was ready to go home, some proud victors and others empty-handed without any land until Clerk Carson discovered an oversight. The leases to the land had been signed on the seventh of the month, so he reasoned they wouldn't be over until midnight of the seventh. Originally he had ruled they would be over by midnight of the sixth. After discovering the mistake, Carson announced to the crowd that today's filings weren't legal. He further explained that he wouldn't open his office until Monday morning at 7:30. At that time, he explained the sale of land would commence again. Half of the crowd was shocked and upset because they had already bought land. The other half was jubilant because now they had another chance to buy some acres for the first time.

The Six Ranch Boys went to San Angelo for recruits. They brought in some muscular, big men to help them. Word was out that each man cost about ten dollars, and it was known that they spent about $150 getting help.

Meantime, the other side of the competition was finding help. Filing applications turned out to be a test of brute strength on Monday morning. At the break of day, Sixers strapped themselves atop the window ledge like the men before them. As the opposition entered, a real hand-to-hand fight ensued. The Sherwood Gang had more muscle as could be clearly seen. Many onlookers, boys and girls alike, cheered as the locals grabbed the Sixers and threw them to the end of the line, or over the side of the chute so they'd be out of the way. They didn't stop there. Two hired muscular men sat on each cowboy that bit the dirt until the second round of the rush was over.

T. S. Sharpe, an observer, later told a newspaper reporter how amazed he was at the athletic ability of some of the smaller men. He said they must have been football players or wrestlers because "some of those fellows would catch great big men, give them a swing and pitch them into the air. He said when they hit the ground you could hear them grunt from a distance of one hundred yards or more." Those people standing by watching decided the fighting guys wanted land a lot more than they did.

The sheriff, Johnny Murphy, stayed in view, but the shear numbers of men involved would have made arrest difficult if tempers had gotten to the point that they had to be made. The Sherwoodites proved to be the victors of the second round.

Men talked for weeks about the land rush. L.C. Fisher told his friends in San Angelo, "I wouldn't have missed it for $1,000 in gold." He later remarked, "I wouldn't participate in another one for $2,000." He explained that the pace was too rowdy for most. He believed that taking pictures of the rush would've been worth more money to him than the land he bought.

Fisher described the land he purchased in the rush by saying, "My 1,280 acres are hung on the side of a steep hill, and will have to be nailed in place during a high wind in order to keep them from sliding into the valley below."

Fisher said that Saturday was fun, but Monday got rather nasty. About fourteen times he charged the line trying to get in front. Each time a big, muscular man would grab him and throw him out saying, "Sit there baby." Usually the man would then flatten him out and sit on Fisher so he couldn't move. He continued by saying, "I grew weary and watched another guy getting thrown out also. This guy had a bald head. Every time he'd enter the line, they'd grab him and toss him out, head first with his pate shining."

A week after the land rush, the newspaper in San Angelo was still writing about the controversy of two different days. Men who had purchased land both days thought they owned it, so the court rulings were used to make final decisions.

The Supreme Court ruling of Hazel and Commissioner Regan indicated that the Irion County lands were not on the market March 7, 1903.

However, the case of McGee and Corbin, which was in nearby Schleicher County, ruled "that land was on the market on expiration of the day of the date, because parties who held the lease and the Commissioner of the General Land Office, by their acts, treated the leases as expiring on such date.

One ruling favored Saturday and the other Monday. Men wrote the Land Commissioner before the rush because they weren't sure when the leases terminated. The following letter was one of the several that Commissioner Terrell sent to inquiring ranchers before the land rush took place.

Mr. Frank Parks

Box 6

Knickerbocker, Texas

Dear Sir:

Replying to your letter of the 17th, beg to advise that land 22629 will expire Mar. 7, 1903 at midnight, and an application to purchase any lands embraced in said lease filed with the clerk prior to that date will not be legal.

Yours truly,

John J. Terrell

This correspondence before the land rush indicates that Terrell would rule the Saturday's sales invalid. Monday's victors were recorded as the official purchasers in the Irion County Records. Only a few men were able to purchase land on Monday as well as Saturday. The Sherwoodites had the upper hand Monday as the tables were turned.

This battle wasn't any worse than the impending fight between Sherwood residents and Mertzon residents as Mertzon began to emerge as an active community.

Chapter 5 – A Loud Ruckus: Sherwood versus Mertzon

In 1889 Sherwoodites had no problems with nonexistent Mertzon, but alfalfa hay raised on some of the farms in Sherwood developed a good problem: they made a lot of hay. After several cuttings, one acre totaled 7.5 tons of fodder. This yield produced a value of $90 an acre, so hay was very profitable to sell. Different kinds of hay could also be put in stacks and fed over a long period of time.

D. S. Gentry was a horse trader who raised hay on one of the farms. He bought a matching team of black horses in 1906, which would bring a good price if they were fattened up a bit. He pitched a large haystack for the horses to eat and put them in the lot with the hay at the time winter showed up. By spring the horses had eaten a tunnel through the stack. Gentry said that the horses brought a pretty fair price.

The Upper Ditch Company now boasted of having 320 acres irrigated in 1906 and declared that it was owned by 20 stockholders. Collecting dues from the ditch members became serious business in 1912 because the Ditch Company decided to collect enough money to build a concrete dam at the mouth of the ditch. This new dam was to replace the log and rock dams, which washed out every time the creek got on a rise.

The location for the new dam was about one mile south of Sherwood and near present Mertzon. A grand total of $570 was collected to build the dam. Gravel was purchased and engineer H. P. Howe was paid $3 a day to serve as foreman while building the dam. Even though it seemed like a super

The Upper Ditch Co. helped to develop Sherwood. Upper photo: the ditch. Lower: Dam east of Mertzon built in 1912. Author's collection.

structure to the citizens around Sherwood, nobody knew if it would hold when the rains brought a heavy flow. Preston Dudley said, "Every time the river flooded, people would say, 'The dam's gone, its gone for sure.' But the water would eventually recede and to everybody's surprise, the dam would still be there." At the time the author wrote this story, the dam is still in place.

After building this magnificent dam, the founding fathers began to realize that they didn't own the land on either side of the dam, nor did they own the land where the ditch flowed out of the dam. Sounds like they got the cart before the horse, doesn't it? "How do we get a hold of the land?" the ditch stockholders must have said. It just happened that the east side of the river, where the ditch flowed, was owned by Fayette Tankersley and the west side of the river was owned by Duwain Hughes. These men could have made life miserable for the Ditch boys by raising the price on this land by the river. If the water from the dam had been stopped, much of the prosperity of Sherwood would have disappeared.

Fayette Tankersley had continued to ranch and develop a farm of his own south of Sherwood. Duwain Hughes came to this area in 1906, homesteaded a ranch and operated a farm in Sherwood. He was a surveyor as well as a rancher with big dreams. Each of these men who held the future of the Upper Ditch Company in their hands had agricultural ties of their own.

A strange turn of event probably acted in the Ditch Company's favor. They were probably saved by the coming of the railroad. Everybody around Sherwood became aware that a railroad was coming through their area. Although a small village, called Mertz, existed at this time on the west side of the river, the consensus of opinions was that the railroad would pass through Sherwood. Since Sherwood was the county seat, it had more people than Mertz did. It was the reasonable place for the train to have its station. Men representing the railroad began trying to buy right-of-way land so the train could come to Sherwood. Some of the upright citizens of this town played hard-to-get with the railroad representative. Meaning that they didn't want to sell their land too cheap to the railroad men, so they held out for a better price.

Then a strange turn of events took place. The railroad men were reminded by citizens of Mertz that the train wouldn't have to cross the river twice if it came straight from San Angelo to Mertz and then to Barnhart, a town about 25 miles southwest of Mertz. In fact, it wouldn't have to cross the river at all. The railroad company would save money was the argument of the "West of the river group."

A Park Land & Cattle Company had been formed and Hughes, as a member, helped to buy 1,200 acres of land near Spring Creek in 1910. This Company gave 600 acres to the Orient Railroad as an incentive to lay track on the west side of the river. This proposal excluded Sherwood of course.

This move by the Park Land & Cattle Company made the free land on the west side of the river very attractive to the railroad men. They wouldn't have to buy right-of-ways or build bridges over Spring Creek. Park Land & Cattle Company had successfully pulled the railway over to the west side of the river. The construction of the railroad was completed about 1912.

A few businesses had already sprung up on the west side of the river. This community was called Mertz after landowner and railroad director of the KCM&O Railroad, M.L. Mertz. The post office later changed the town's name to avoid confusion with a town already called "Mertz" so Mertzon was born.

Early stores in Mertzon included a mercantile store started by Mack and Tom Woods. Sam Oglesby provided a much-needed livery stable. The Lewis Hotel, formerly in Sherwood, was divided into two parts, pulled across the river by teams of horses and put back together. This feat was accomplished on this large two-storied hotel by placing many poles under the structure parallel to each other. When the horses moved the building several feet forward, poles were left behind the building. These were moved to the front of the building and arranged to hold up that end of the hotel. This procedure was repeated many times until the hotel reached its destination. A Presbyterian church was the first house of God to appear in Mertzon. Several different denominations used this building in the first years of the town's existence. By 1910 a second hotel, the Brock Hotel, moved from Sherwood to Mertzon. Some citizens of the area were surprised as building after building made the move across the river to the new town. This new community soon had a Model T taxi service furnished by A.M. Callison.

The Upper Ditch Company may not have been aware that the development of Mertzon hinged on their continued success Their vegetables, hay and cotton from the farms was needed by the new town because most of the good farm land was on the east side of the river. Mertzon didn't have many

The Lewis Hotel in present day Mertzon. It was divided into two parts and moved from Sherwood to Mertzon. Author's collection.

Oglesby Feed & Wagon Yard at Mertzon. Courtesy of the West Texas Collection, Angelo State Univ.

farms on their side of Spring Creek, so their citizens needed the produce raised on the farms. Hughes and Tankersley readily sold right-of-way acreage to the Upper Ditch Company in

1912 because these two men "had bigger fish to fry." They were building a town.

But for the Ditch Boys, life seemed great. After the celebration of building the dam and having the deed to the ditch land, the Upper Ditch had another high point; they received the Water Rights from the State of Texas' 33rd Legislature in 1914. Battles were over for the Ditch Company. Sherwood residents thought their irrigation system was secure and so was their town.

Children during this time didn't worry about the town problems. Instead, they enjoyed fishing, making whistles out of the willow branches or racing their "boats" in the ditch. Now these "boats" were Mom's washtub and the paddles used in washing clothes were their "oars." Teenagers switched their attention from the ditch to the watermelons growing in the fields nearby. Many a juicy, ripe melon was stolen. If the guilty party lived very far from the melon patch, they would roll the melon into the ditch and float it down to their home in Sherwood according to Jake Cox. He probably tried this a few times himself.

The water around Mertzon and Sherwood also held an interest to another group of young people. Those of dating age dressed in their Sunday best and after church they walked with friends along the river. If it was a pretty day, my mother Laverne Gentry, said that "kodaking" was popular even in the 1930s.

Many a snapshot was made of a group standing on the water's edge and enjoying the shade of big pecan and oak trees. If the weather was warm, swimming was also enjoyed. Girls could swim, but they must keep on their stockings even when in the water. When an Irion County girl decided to be daring and swam without her stockings, one of her male cousins came to the water's edge and warned her, "You had better put on your stockings. They are arresting girls who did this in Galveston." Preston Dudley remembered this exchange between cousins.

More important happenings were the appearance of the railroad track. The railroad ties were laid on the west side of Spring Creek and the first passenger train came through Mertzon in 1911. With the train came the development of the town. The First National Bank of Mertzon was organized by Fayette Tankersley, who was the first bank president. In 1909 a large two-storied school building made from native stone was constructed in Mertzon. It set west of the railroad about five blocks from downtown Mertzon. One could almost see the businesses and the people sliding from the east side of the river at Sherwood to the west side in Mertzon.

How a new school in Sherwood was financed is a subject of debate. Supposedly bonds were voted on in November of 1914. The two-stored Sherwood school building was completed in 1915. It included ten grades and had a nice auditorium on the second floor. Troy Williams lived in Sherwood at the time the school was built. He had heard that railroad money helped build it.

Sherwood continued as the county seat of Irion County for quite a few more years. Sherwood had been the county seat of Irion County since the origination of the county in March of 1889. Their own two-storied courthouse was spacious and took care of county needs. Plus they had a separate two-storied jail.

Some of the county officials were quite interesting. Dave S. Gentry, the horse trader, was County Tax Assessor from 1915 to 1922. He had teenage daughters, Nora and Myrtle, who were very good at helping him keep the tax rolls. One hot afternoon his daughters thought Dad needed their help, so they looked for him in the courthouse. They asked a man in an office nearby if he had seen their Dad. "Yep," he said, "He's out yonder sleeping in the courtyard under a tree." Sure enough, the girls found their Dad under the tree fast asleep. Seems that his office was on the northwest corner of the courthouse, a place where no air circulated during the summer. Dave Gentry's behavior didn't seem to hurt him because he was elected County Judge a few years later.

During the 1920s and 1930s, Mertzon continued to grow in population. They began to have "city" rules such as rounding up any stray animals and putting them in the city pound. Common knowledge circulating around Sherwood stated that the Mertzon pound man drove stock from Sherwood where there was "free range" for livestock to his corral in Mertzon so he could charge a pound fee. This action made some people of Sherwood very mad because they had to pay the fee and bring their livestock home.

Dave S. Gentry, horse trader, Tax-Assessor, and later County judge.
Author's collection.

Creed and Lillie Childress lived in Sherwood and always had some horses. Creed often worked out of town for days at a time building roads, fences or dirt tanks on the surrounding ranches. Lillie was left to tend to the animals when he was away. After two weeks of missing two of her horses, Lillie was upset. She didn't have a car to use in looking for them. Finally her nephew, Richard Reed, saw the horses in the Mertzon pound.

When he told Lillie he saw the horses locked up with no feed or water, she was fit to be tied. This mild five-feet four little woman began to plan the way she'd get her horses. She always wore dresses and was feminine by nature. However, this particular night was to be different. Lillie waited until dark, then she put on her husband's overalls, shirt and hat. Her nephew came for her and drove her to the pound. Once there she used pliers to cut the fence and then she drove her horses home to Sherwood.

No shots were ever fired over the "animal pound" incident, but feelings between the two towns weren't on the friendly side. Mertzon was growing and wanted the courthouse in their town. Finally in April of 1927 an election was held to move the county seat to Mertzon. The Sherwood Courthouse was only 26 years old at this time. Citizens of the two towns were very verbal toward each other and feelings ran high before the election. The results at the ballot box showed that 286 people voted to move the county seat and 231 voted against it. People of Sherwood sighed with relief because Mertzon didn't get the necessary two-thirds vote. Sherwood still had their courthouse.

But Mertzon hadn't given up yet. On September 7, 1936, they had another election. This time the results were different. Those voting for the change were 453 and only 212 people voted against the move. The new town of Mertzon was jubilant. They'd won. Sherwoodites still had some fight left in them. They contested the election because it had been less than the mandatory ten years between the two elections. The case of Cal Rutledge versus R. J. Atkinson went to court, but Mertzon won. Sherwood carried the case to the Texas Supreme Court, but Mertzon won again.

Bitter words were spoken both before and after the decree of the courts. Men who had hunted together and worked side by side became enemies. At this point, Sherwood was reduced to two or three businesses, two churches and the school. As the school decreased in enrollment, few were surprised at the election results, which consolidated the two schools in 1946. Technically, Sherwood had school for one more year. A student, L.D. White, needed one more year to graduate from Sherwood. If he moved to Mertzon, he would have two or more years before he could graduate because the programs were different. To help this student, teacher Marvin Carr agreed to teach him for a year, and he did, according to L. D.'s daughter Elaine Halley. Her Dad graduated on time.

When the schools moved to Mertzon, it was the final blow to the community of Sherwood. This little community became a ghost town of sorts. The farming in the area has continued, but farmers grow mostly hay and permanent grazing. The dam at Mertzon has held, and the irrigation system has been in existence for over 120 years.

But in 2005, a startling thing happened to the ditch company. The Texas Quality Environmental Control received complaints that the members of the Upper Ditch Company were using more than their share of the water in Spring Creek. Those people complaining had property on Spring Creek below the Upper Ditch Company. According to the 1914 water rights, the Upper Ditch Company had one permit to use 596 acre feet of water. In 2005, this water was distributed between 22 landowners.

The State of Texas sent a Water Master to monitor the flow of water in the ditches since their permit called for a maximum diversion flow rate of 10 cubic feet per second. Some farmers went to the water meetings provided by the state and other didn't. It seemed like the uninformed people thought the ditch officers were making the whole thing up. Tempers flared. The Ditch Boss in 2006 got into trouble because it was his job to see that the ditches were cleaned. One farmer didn't want him on his property, so he had the Sheriff put the Ditch Boss in the jail. Of course, he only stayed a bit, but the whole thing got out of hand.

As of 2006, the Water Master controlled the gate where the water flows out of Spring Creek. The amount of water that the ditch company actually gets is so small that all the acre-feet of water allowed for a year according to their permit was used up in 30 days. The dam on Spring Creek is one mile from the farms, so the dirt ditch soaks up too much of the water. Farmers who pump from the river also have to have meters, so the irrigation time is severely limited for everyone.

Aside from water problems, the area is doing very well. Mertzon is a small town, but it's a vigorous community that depends on oil and ranching for its livelihood. Since city lots in a ghost town are less expensive than in other places, many people are moving to Sherwood so they can enjoy the tranquility of the area. They can also keep an eye on the old courthouse. Some repair work is being done to the beautiful old limestone building at this time. In the 1880s, outlaws were a problem.

Chapter 6 – Outlaw's Ruckus: Black Jack Ketchum

At the tender age of eighteen, young "Black Jack" Ketchum had his first hideout. And it was near the nice little village of Knickerbocker, Texas. By age thirty-six, he and his gang were wanted for sixteen murders and too many train robberies to count. During that span of time, he occupied many different caves and hideouts in Texas and New Mexico, to name a few.

Young Tom, or Black Jack as he was later called, was born October 31, 1863. His parents, Green Berry Ketchum and his wife, Constance, tried to scratch out a living on a small farm a few miles west of San Saba, Texas. Other older children in the family were Nancy, Sam and eldest, Berry. Their parents died when Tom was only nine years old.

Twenty-year old Berry took over the chore of raising three younger siblings. As he worked on nearby ranches, many times he left the younger children alone. Maurine Duncan Atkinson, grandniece of Tom Ketchum, remembered family stories about the Ketchum children's years alone. She said, "When Berry was gone, the children would wash their plates in the creek. Once a metal dish started to float away, so Nancy tied a rope around little Tom. He swam out in the river, retrieved it and was pulled back to the bank safely. They were so poor that one dish was an important possession."

Life continued to be tough as the kids were older. They worked wherever they could. As a teen-ager, Tom worked as a hand on cattle ranches at nearby Richland Springs. There was evidence that he and brother Sam did their first cattle rustling in San Saba County. By riding Berry's racehorses the brothers kept one jump ahead of the law.

Brother Berry started a horse and cattle ranch near Knickerbocker, which is southwest of San Angelo. His siblings made the move with him in 1880. At the age of eighteen, Tom had his first hideout about five miles south of Berry's new ranch. It was little more than a rock overhang, which sheltered them from the elements. An old rock nearby bears the date "Sept. 81" in the gully near this hideout. The rock has figures, numbers and letters scratched in it. Supposedly, if a person could understand the symbols, they could find the buried treasure, which the young men hid. This early day graffiti included initials "WSK and WHC." WHC stood for William Carver, and WSK stood for Sam Ketchum. Tom already had assembled his gang at this early age. About two miles south of this hideout was a large table-top mountain. Legend has it that the teenagers used it for a lookout because when they were on top of it, they could see in every direction for ten or more miles.

Sometimes the weather was so bad that Tom had to come home even though he and older brother Berry didn't see eye to eye. Instead of coming to Berry's house, Tom slipped into the Ketchum bunkhouse on these wintry nights. Joseph Schmidt was a cowboy on the Berry Ranch. His son Carl Schmidt related the story that his Dad told on Tom. Joseph said that sometimes he would be asleep in the bunkhouse when he could hear Tom

The author sitting on a rock near the overhang that served as a hideout for Black Jack.

say, "Move over. I'm gettin' in bed with you, Joseph." At that time the older cowpuncher knew that the youngun had frozen out.

Big brother didn't always agree with Tom's lifestyle. When Berry was leaving to go back to San Saba to get his bride, he gave Tom an ultimatum, "Be out of the house for good when I return." Tom was riled by this show of authority. He left his brother's house, but he departed on the back of his brother's best racehorse.

Tom drifted northwest the next ten years, but reappeared in West Texas now and then. Col. Jack Potter met Tom in

Carlsbad, New Mexico in 1890 and gave this description of the youngest Ketchum: "Tom was a big, handsome fellow with raven black hair, a swarthy complexion and a meticulously cared-for mustache. He made a striking picture with his flashing black eyes." In 1891 Tom worked for the Carrizozo Cattle Company and later for Frank Garst of the G-G brand. Both ranches were in New Mexico. The year 1894 found him working in northern Colorado.

Tom Ketchum, a sketch used by the Pinkerton Detectives to catch outlaws.

Tom made two trips back home to Knickerbocker during the 1890s. One was on the lighter side; seems Tom made a quick visit to church. He was chasing a dog out in the street, and it ran into the church door while Sunday services were in progress. Tom followed him into the crowded church much to the dismay of the congregation.

The other trip back to Knickerbocker became a more serious matter. Tom Ketchum, Dave Atkins and Bud Upshaw were given murder indictments by the Tom Green County grand jury for the death of John N. "Jap" Powers, a Knickerbocker farmer. Supposedly, this murder happened December 12, 1895. Powers was looking for his horse, which had a bell on it. The three men hid in a thicket, rang the bell and shot Powers when he investigated the sound of the bell. Tom could not be found after the indictment because he had the racehorse headed toward New Mexico.

According to Frank Shelton, a Texas sheriff of Martin and Midland counties, Tom took the name Black Jack from Jack Gregg. He was an old-time outlaw who disappeared into Mexico. Other sources say Tom got the name from cutting black jack trees. According to tales told, he could cut'em pretty fast.

Tom also had a hideout in Irion County west of Mertzon. Another hill in that area also bears the name "Ketchum Mountain." One time the sheriff of Irion County took his wife out west of town on a Sunday afternoon buggy ride. Several days later, Tom told the sheriff, "I had you and your misses in my sights all afternoon. Better not take her west of town again because my gun might go off."

Black Jack had two sides to his personality. At the first of his outlaw days, he paid for what he stole. He came riding into the Bar-N Ranch in western Socorro County, New Mexico in the late 1890's. Tom demanded three fresh horses and threw $320 on the ground as payment. However, when strangers refused to pass him the butter in a restaurant, he pulled his six-shooter out and demanded they eat all the butter. Then he had the waiter bring another pound of butter for them to eat. Robert W. Lewis was a neighbor of the Ketchum boys and later a New Mexico lawman. He said, "Black Jack was the most cold-blooded individual I have ever met and would not hesitate to kill a man or even a boy."

A prominent investigator and prosecutor for the New Mexico Stock Growers Association, Col. Albert Fountain, was leaving court in Lincoln County New Mexico, February 1, 1896. Traveling with him was his eight-year old son. Fountain had just gotten 32 indictments for cattle theft that day. A note of warning given to him earlier in the day said that the attorney's life was in danger, but this didn't stop him from traveling a lonely road home. Fountain could have requested a lawman's escort, but he didn't. Legend has it that three horsemen followed him that day. On a lonely stretch of road outside of Las Cruces, both father and son's bodies were later found dead. Lawmen hunted for the killers but never brought anyone to trial. Black Jack's gang was accused of this killing.

By the spring of 1897, Black Jack was back in Texas near the Mexican border. Will Carver, who had run a saloon in San Angelo with Black Jack's brother Sam, was riding with Tom. Dave Atkins who was indicted in the Jap Powers murder was also with them. The outlaws held up the Southern Pacific train when it stopped at Lozier, between Dryden and Langtry on May 14, 1897. The three men climbed aboard, stopped the train and dynamited two safes that were on board. When both safes exploded, the robbers grabbed $42,000. An elderly woman on the train asked what was happening as she stuck her head out the train window. Ketchum replied, "Get your head back in

The Ketchums made these markings in a cave that was 10 miles downriver from Pandale, Texas. They may have stayed there before the train holdups.

there, Grandma."

She replied, "Young man, you keep a civil tongue in your head." After this heist, the gang was seen in Knickerbocker. Rumor had it that Ketchum's gang hid some of their loot in Black Jack's sister's house. They hid it in a trunk. Some time later, that house burned down and the loot was destroyed.

A month or two later, Tom, Carver and Atkins returned to New Mexico. They picked up Sam Ketchum and lived in a boarding house in Cimarron. This life was quite different than the hilltop lookouts and caves where they generally lived. Two hideouts with mountain lookouts were known near their home in Knickerbocker. They also had a hideout in Arizona.

When the gang showed lots of gambling money there in Cimarron, they drew suspicious glances from the local gents. Black Jack decided they better leave town. They found a shallow cave in Turkey Creek Canyon, ten miles northwest of Cimarron. Years later, someone made a picture of this cave, It set on a hillside about four feet from the trail that went by the opening. According to the picture, you had to climb up the hillside to get to the opening. Using logs they made a barricade near the cave and fashioned a corral close to a stream. It's possible this cave reminded Black Jack of one he had used near Eldorado, Texas. That hideout was about 35 miles from Knickerbocker, and it had running water in it. Black Jack taught his horse to nicker when someone was in sight. When Tom hid in this cave, his horse told him if danger was nearby.

After fixing the New Mexico hideout for their new home, Black Jack's gang was ready for another robbery. The four men; two Ketchums, Will Carver and Dave Atkins, struck a train at Folsum again. This time it was a Denver and Gulftian train, which left Folsum about 10 p.m. It was the night of September 3, 1897. Two outlaws got on the train while the other two held the horses further down the track. The safe and most of the express car was blown. This haul amounted to four to five thousand dollars.

In 1898 and 1899, there were seven train robberies or attempted robberies in New Mexico. The state had passed a law that train robberies would be given the death sentence. The new law didn't stop Black Jack.

He just started another train robbery spree in Texas. On April 28, 1898, Tom, Sam, Will Carver and Dave Atkins robbed a train between Langtry and Del Rio. They received an unknown amount of money. Their next hit was between Stanton and Midland. When they blew the passenger car with the safe, it also got the express car. There were two rewards: they got $500 currency and all the watermelons they wanted to eat came blowing out of the express car. Train riders watched as the robbers sat on the train track eating melons.

Ketchum and his gang drifted back to New Mexico. The Folsom holdup seemed like an ideal spot, so on July 11, 1899, they hit it for a second time. Sheriff Ed Parr and his posse followed them to their Turkey Creek hideout. After 45 minutes of gun battle, five of the posse were dead, including Parr. Sam Ketchum was captured and died of blood poisoning soon there after.

A friend of Black Jack's, Jack Potter, rode with him for three years. He recalled how Tom had this one girlfriend, known only as Cora, who lived near Fort Stanton. Once a year, he would visit her. On the third visit, Tom told Cora, "We'll get married, go up on the Ruidoso, get a squatter's cabin and build a nest. We'll live happily ever after." She assured him he was the only one for her. Later, Cora wrote Tom that she had eloped with C. G. Slim. In the letter, she told Tom that he had taught her how to lie. Shortly after reading the letter, Tom drew his pay, saddled his horse and left.

It's possible that this girlfriend episode added to his moodiness. Black Jack continued to be brutal and increasingly violent. Those people around him noticed that he took to hitting his head when things didn't go right. One by one, his gang left him.

On the night of August 16, 1899, all of his gang members had left him, so Tom decided to holdup the C & S train at Folsum by himself. Frank E. Harrington, the conductor on the train, had a different idea. Harrington had taken out a $10, 000 life insurance policy himself. As he loaded his shotgun with 00 buckshot, he told his wife, "Well, if they try to hold up the train again, I'll either kill them or they'll kill me. They've held us up twice now, and I'm getting tired of it."

As the train stopped once more, Harrington slipped through the cars so he could see the robbers. Black Jack and Harrington saw each other the same time and opened fire. Harrington had a flesh wound, but Black Jack had his arm blasted with buckshot above the elbow. He staggered away in the darkness. Saturnino Pinard, sheriff of Union County, took the next train through and found Black Jack about 300 yards from the track.

Black Jack was put in a hospital and told that his arm would have to be amputated. He tried to kill himself, so they took him to the New Mexico Penitentiary, August 24, 1899. Amputation took place on September 3, 1899. Black Jack's health improved after the operation, so he tried to escape. A trial was held, and Black Jack pleaded guilty to train robbery.

He was held in prison in Santa Fe for a year to be tried for other crimes, including the death of 16 men. After his conviction, he was sent to Clayton for execution. An enclosed hanging scaffold was set, and 150 seats were arranged to see the gruesome event   Tickets were sold to see the hanging.

Black Jack's last minute advice was "To the boys of the country is not to steal horses or sheep but either rob a train or a bank when you get to be an outlaw and every man who came in your way, kill him; spare no mercy for they will show you none. That is the way I feel about it, and I think I feel right about it." Then to the hangman he said, "Let'er rip."

When Black Jack was hung, April 26, 1901, the hangman misjudged the drop, and Black Jack was decapitated. After sewing his head on, he was placed in a simple pine box. Black Jack was laid to rest in a cemetery one mile east of town with no service or mourners. In 1933, his body was moved to Clayton Cemetery in town.

While Black Jack was roaming the Concho country, two other outlaws who once were in Ketchum's gang were hitting the robber's trail. Ben Kilpatrick and Laura Bullion were moving.

Black Jack's hanging in Clayton, New Mexico was quite a spectacle.

When outlaws robbed people, they didn't want these tokens.
Merchants in small towns used them as change.

Chapter 7 – More Outlaw Ruckuses

One family who made it to the Dove Creek area before 1879 and played a major part in the outlaw scenario was the Byler Family. It wasn't the elder Byler's intent to raise the outlaw population of the area because Elliot and Serena Byler were law-abiding citizens themselves. Their children were Fereby, Jake, Laura and Mary.

Elliot and Serena Byler farmed and lived on Dove Creek in 1879 because a *San Angelo Standard Times* article mentioned them selling some $840 worth of vegetables. They were also listed on the 1880 Census of Tom Green where they moved from Washington County, Arkansas. The older couple didn't have much time to enjoy having their children grown and gone because around 1881, their daughter, Fereby Byler Bullion, brought her children back to live with them.

Fereby had married J. Henry Bullion in 1875 and had children named Laura, Dan and Fannie Lee. It isn't known whether she and J. Henry divorced or if he died. Fereby left the children with their grandparents and was reported to have married a man named Scott for awhile. However, she left him to later return to Dove Creek and live the rest of her life with her parents. Meanwhile her daughter Laura had skipped the country.

The Elliott Byler ranch was about eight miles east of Sherwood and six miles west of Knickerbocker, so they were involved with activities in both communities. Fereby died as a young woman, and her grave is in the Sherwood Cemetery. The tombstone reads "Fereby Byler Bullion, 1858 – 1891."

Lack of a mother probably added to the problems that young Laura Bullion had. But her older grandmother tried to make her become a nice little lady. She taught her how to cook and sew. Schooling was provided either in Knickerbocker or in Sherwood. However, an Aunt Viana Byler who was only two years older than Laura seemed to influence her most.

When Viana was only seventeen, she fell in love with a cowboy named Will Carver, and they married in 1891. He worked on ranches near San Angelo and Sonora, Texas. Will was a friend of Sam and Tom Ketchum. Sam and Will developed a partnership and ran a saloon in San Angelo for a short time. Viana died a year after the marriage, and Will began to be more interested in activities outside the law rather than ranch work.

Laura had met Will earlier, and when Viana died, he seemed to take up with her, probably because she looked a little like Viana. However, pictures of Viana show her as much prettier than Laura. Once Laura decided to follow the boys, sometimes she stayed in their camp and sometime she stayed at the Byler ranch. Besides knowing the Ketchums, Will also ran with Ben and George Kilpatrick of Concho County. Many times the boys would be on the run and hungry. They'd ride to a thicket of trees near the Byler ranch and signal to Laura that they were there. She'd take food out to them. During this time, the robberies they committed were often along the Pecos River where the lonely stretches of train track existed.

On one such venture, Kilpatrick, along with the Ketchums robbed a train and put the gold bars in a wagon. They brought the wagon back to Christoval where Ben's sister Alice lived. After supper the men took the wagon out of Christoval and were gone about an hour. Supposedly, the treasure was buried nearby. Curious treasure seekers did find fresh sign in a nearby draw where a set of wagon wheels left tracks, but they never found the treasure.

A sketch of Laura Bullion while she was still at home with her grandparents. The artist is Sharon Gentry

People who knew Laura saw the change in her. Knickerbocker neighbors like Joseph Tweedy would tell the Bylers, "If you don't watch that girl, she'll run off." Laura did finally leave the Concho country and lived in San Antonio during the years 1891 to 1893. This action suggests that she left home soon after her mother's death. In San Antonio, she worked as a prostitute most likely because one of her most used aliases in later years was Della Rose. She probably got this name from a street in San Antonio where a popular brothel was located, Fanny Porter's Sporting House on the corner of Military Avenue and Delarosa Street.

While Laura was in San Antonio, Ben and George Kilpatrick from Concho County threw in with Will Carver and began robbing, about 1896 or 1897. They rode some with the Ketchums. On March 27, 1901, these three with Harvey Logan (Kid Curry) were playing croquet at the Kilpatrick home in Concho County.

A neighbor, Oliver Thornton, came to the house and told the boys he was having a hard time raising any crops because the Kilpatrick hogs were in his fields. An argument developed and Thornton was killed, then the law was on their trail again.

When the group went to Eldorado, they posed as polo horse buyers. Next they entered Sonora to buy some feed. Sheriff E. S. Briant was tipped off and killed Will Carver. George Kilpatrick was badly wounded in the gunfight. When Laura was later arrested in St. Louis, she had letters that Will had written to her in her possession. One letter was written from Sherwood, Texas, and the other one was posted from Ponca City, Oklahoma. A notebook of hers also had this inscription:

> W. R. Carver, killed Tuesday April 2, 1901. He has fled. I wish him dead, he that wrought my ruin. O, the flattery and the craft, which were my undoing.

When Ben Kilpatrick left Sonora, he had Laura Bullion with him. Ben, often called "The Tall Texan," might have felt responsible for his dead partner's girl friend or maybe he'd had his eye on her all along. The two outlaws spent some time in Fort Worth before heading to Montana to meet with the Wild Bunch: Robert Leroy Parker (Butch Cassidy), Harry Longabaugh (the Sundance Kid), Elza Lay and other outlaws.

On July 3, 1901, near Wagner, Montana the gang held up the Northern Pacific Train. The loot was $150,000 in unsigned bank notes of First National Bank of Helena, Montana. A few weeks later, Ben Kilpatrick and Laura were caught in St. Louis with $100,000 of the bills. Ben was given 10 years and Laura was given five years because she held the horses and assisted in the robbery.

She corresponded with Ben after the sentencing, even though they were in different prisons. He was in a federal prison in Atlanta, Georgia while she was in the Missouri State Penitentiary at Jefferson City, Missouri. Every other Sunday, she wrote letters to Ben and to his family. She didn't correspond with her own family, though. She heard news about her family only through letters she received from the Kilpatricks.

Although Laura wrote upbeat letters and tried to comfort Ben, he seemed more demanding in his correspondence. He always wanted something for himself and wallowed in self-pity.

Laura worked as a prison nurse and got out after only three years in prison because of good behavior. She immediately hurried to Atlanta where Ben was still imprisoned. A week after getting out of prison, Laura bought half interest in a rooming house in Atlanta. Where the money came from to make this purchase could only be speculated. She may have carried on prostitution successfully during this time.

Laura intended to stay there until Ben was released, but reporters and investigators harassed her so much that she finally moved to Birmingham, Alabama. When Ben finally was let go, authorities ushered him back to Texas to try him for the Thornton murder in Concho County. Laura came back to Texas also and was present at the court proceedings. When he was acquitted, she and Ben finally got to be together as they went to Ben's brother's ranch near Sheffield, Texas. Their bliss was short lived.

Ben Kilpatrick dressed like a city slicker when the Wild Bunch made their Ft. Worth photo in 1901.

Frank Hobeck had met Ben in prison. On March 12, 1912, Ben, Frank, Butch Cassidy and the Sundance Kid decided to rob the train as it pulled into Dryden, Texas. Two of the gang climbed aboard in Dryden, stuck a gun in the ribs of Engineer Grosh and Fireman Holmes, and told them to stop up the tracks a little ways out of town. Unknown to the robbers, David Andrew Trousdale was inside the baggage car. Frank Hobeck found Trousdale and the rest of the crew. He frisked them and returned them to the mail car. In the next step, the passenger cars were uncoupled and left in the desert as Kilpatrick in the engine told them to move away from the passenger car. Trousdale realized he and helper Reagan were outnumbered, so he began to gripe that Wells Fargo didn't pay him enough to protect their money.

Trousdale's whining caught Hobeck off guard. The bandit leaned his gun on the side of the car and looked at the loot that Trousdale pointed out to him. While Hobeck was adsorbed with the money, Trousdale grabbed an ice mallet and killed Hobeck. Then the trainmen had to get Kilpatrick. Trousdale took the two pistols off the dead Hobeck and gave them to Reagan and the mail clerk, Mr. Bank. Armed with the bandit's Winchester, he sat down with the other two men to wait for the robber on the outside of the train to climb aboard. Time went by and nobody came inside. Finally the Wells Fargo guard, Trousdale, became impatient and fired a shot through the railroad car roof.

From outside the train a voice said, "Frank? Frank?" Then Kilpatrick finally opened the door to see what was happening inside the train car. Trousdale killed him with one shot. The Wells Fargo man had deadly aim because his bullet found his target. The bullet went in "The Tall Texan's" left eye, out the back of his head and into the wall of the train. At 5 a.m. the next morning in the town of Sanderson, horrible pictures were made of the dead bandits. The two corpses were propped up at the train station and photographed for a grisly picture that would be seen on the front page of many newspapers. This event marked the last train robbery on the Sunset Route.

Now Laura Bullion felt more alone than ever. Her grandfather Byler was dead and her grandmother was being cared for by family members. Mrs. Byler was up in her eighties. Laura's own sister, Fanny Lee, had disowned the family and couldn't be counted on to help Laura. After Ben Kilpatrick's death, Laura wanted to get out of Texas, but she had no money. Finally in desperation, Laura won the sympathy of her uncle Jake Byler. He gave her enough money to get out of Texas.

She spent the rest of her life in the South. Laura made her living as a seamstress in department stores and drapery shops. From 1924 until her death December 2, 1861, Memphis, Tennessee was her home. Aliases of Freda Lincoln and Freda Arnold were used. In the later part of her life, she suffered from arteriosclerosis and had to depend on friends to bring her a tray of food. Laura would open her front door only wide enough for the food to pass through. She died as a very lonely person.

Although Knickerbocker had the dubious honor of producing the Ketchums and Laura Bullion, life in that area became much calmer after they died. This community now has ranches and farmland, which is still maintained by people who love the land. The little town has a post office and community center housed in the red brick school building and two active churches.

Community spirit has survived among the small group of inhabitants and there's no more ruckuses along the rivers.

Bibliography

Books

Rister, *Robert E. Lee in Texas*

Clements, Gus, *The Concho Country.* San Antonio: Mulberry Avenue Books, 1980.

Crawford, Leta, *Irion County History.* Waco: Texian Press, 1966.

Rutherford, Phillip. *"Disaster at Dove Creek," Civil War Times Illustrated, Vol. 22, No. 1, March 1983.*

Havins, Thomas Roberts, Camp Colorado, A Decade of Frontier Defense, Brownwood, Texas: Brown Press, 1964.

Gibson, Joe, Old Angelo, San Angelo: Educator Books, Inc., 1971.

Van Court, Billie Marie, History of Christoval Baptist Church.

"Thomas Jackson Perciful," New Encyclopedia of Texas.

Tweedy, Jose, Knickerbocker Community Center, Inc. Memorial. "Salome Jacvques, Alvinia Flores Morales, Stephen Dexter Arthur, Boyd Cornick, M.D.; Gilberto Cruz, Barnabe Martinez.

Irion County Historical Society, Irion County History.

Miller, Thomas Lloyd, The Public Lands of Texas 1579 – 1970. Norman: University of Oklahoma Press, 1972

Martin, Lillie Childress, Genealogy of A.D. Hensley 1820 – 1985. California, 1985.

Howard, Byron, Robbers, Rogues, and Ruffins, Santa Fe: Clear Light Publishers, 1991.

"The Last Train Robbery," UnSung Heroes of Texas.

Interviews and Talks

Speech by Dr. Frankie Beth Nelson at Fort Concho, 1994.

Speech by Katherine Waring ,"George W. DeLong," at Tom Green County historical Society meeting April 17, 1978.

Interview with Mildred Kirby 1987.

Interview with Frances Schneider about her mother, Mary Reed, 1995.

Talk by Jose Tweedy , "History of Baze Community ," at Tom Green Historical Society, January 15, 1996.

Interview with Jose Tweedy, June 8, 1996.

Interview with Rose Duke, Aug. 14, 1996.

Interview with Carl Schmidt, Feb. 8, 1995, Nov. 26, 1996; May 14, 1994

.Letter written to the author by William Webb, Jan. 28, 1995.

Interview with Arthur Franco, Aug. 3, 1996.

Interview with Paul Martinez, 1995.

Interview with Nora Locklin, July 10, 1994.

Interviews with Maureen Atkinson, March 13, 1994

Interview with Margaret Crawford, Jan. 1995.

Interview with Mrs. Jake Byler, Jr., Feb. 7, 1995.

Interview with Ed Harris, June 6, 1994

Magazines and Newspapers

Pool, William C., "The Battle of Dove Creek," Southwestern Historical Quarterly , Vol. L111, No. 4, April, 1950.

Waring, Katherine, "The Battle of Dove Creek," San Angelo Standard Times, Oct. 3, 1980.

Waring, Katherine, "The DeLong Family," San Angelo Standard Times, Oct. 23, 1980.

Boggs, Hershal, "A History of Fort Concho."

"And Actiivities Centered around Mire's Rockhouse," San Angelo Standard Times. July 31, 1906.

Milligan, Wilma, "Career of C. Doty," Frontier Times, Vol. 5 No. 7, April 1925.

McBride, "The Thorny Rose," True West, April 1992

Articles from the Standard Times" Nov. 16, 1995; March 5, 1902; Feb. 25, 1902; Mar. 12, 1902; Sept. 21, 1889; Mar. 5, 1891;

Sept. 21, 1889; Mar. 7, 1903; Mar. 14, 1903; Mar. 21, 1903; Oct. 3, 1889; Sept. 14, 1889;

Papers and Manuscripts

McMillan, Clarice Atkins, "History of Christoval, Texas 1874 – 1968. 1968.

Fundersmith, Connie, "Knickerbocker settled with Baze brother's help." Swan Angelo Standard Times. Aug. 13, 1984.

Barton, Barbara, "What's in a name." Toenail Tribune, May 3, 1995.

"R. F. Holt," Verticle Files, West Texas Collection, Angelo State University.

Gill, Judy, "History of Knickerbocker Community Church."

"Black Jack," West Texas Collection vertical files, San Angelo State Univ.

Upper Ditch Co. Minutes 1914.

Index